Paradise Renewed

Paradise Renewed

A Vision of the Last Days
in a Journey to the New Jerusalem

S. J. BEGUELY

RESOURCE *Publications* · Eugene, Oregon

PARADISE RENEWED
A Vision of the Last Days in a Journey to the New Jerusalem

Resource Publications
An Imprint of Wipf and Stock Publishers
199 W. 8th Ave., Suite 3
Eugene, OR 97401

www.wipfandstock.com

PAPERBACK ISBN: 979-8-3852-2627-6
HARDCOVER ISBN: 979-8-3852-2628-3
EBOOK ISBN: 979-8-3852-2629-0

VERSION NUMBER 07/29/24

This book is dedicated to the many believers, Messianic and Gentile, the coming One New Man, who recognize that the glimpses into the eschatological future which the Bible gives are meant to instruct us, and particularly to show us that God's revelation of these matters must be a spur to both the working out of our own salvation, and to the evangelization of the lost. God's primary purpose in these events is not the salvation of a few, but that every possible soul who can be saved will be saved. The mystery of this plan involves the entirety of His creation, culminating in a New Heaven and a New Earth.

I also dedicate it to my wife, Sue, whose exceptional copyediting improves the flow considerably, and whose spiritual insight over the years informs much of the dialogue.

CONTENTS

PREFACE

"Words are like medicine, measure carefully each one, above all, avoid an overdose."

—R. BUNAM PARAPHRASED

The poem *Song of the Beloved*, in a previous book, is the core of this poem. It outlined in a more or less classical rhyming form the sequence of events and the impact of those events in the last days, in accord with the last days synopsis the poem itself was based on. This expansion of that history of the last days, post-history if you like, elaborates the fate of a single man during those times.

Every narrative, in poetry or prose, and especially when of epic proportions, needs a timeline that events and people fit into, so the events of what are called the last days, the eschaton, are mostly here interpreted literally for the sake of the story flow. The reality when it occurs, and even taking our present personal reality as its fulfillment, will no doubt be a mixture of literal fulfillments and symbolic significance, but a good story should be capable of both modes of interpretation.

It should be remembered that although this story is based on a close analysis of the Scriptures, it *is* fiction which adds flesh to the bare bones of the revelation of the Lord Jesus concerning the last days. It does not attempt to add to Scripture, rather to contextualize it for a modern reader. Like the movie series *The Chosen* (with respect to the gospels) it personalizes the events of the last days to increase understanding of the cryptic eschatological events and their long-term significance, both for salvation and our sanctification. I have deliberately sought an economy of words, trying to avoid an overelaboration of the circumstances and events of the last days which would risk becoming unscriptural or improbable or both, as even Milton's inspirational masterpiece *Paradise Lost* did occasionally. It is only one possible creative expression of how the narrative of those times might work out, though it is founded closely on a literal reading of the end-times narrative of Scripture. For the curious, the appendices give a fair summary of the rationale for the timeline.

The dates given in the course of the story and its headers are, like all the details propounded, merely a contextualization for our times. In a hundred years' time a publisher might change them to roughly match their own era, and that would be a true rendering, because it would preserve the all-important and pervasive element of imminence.

ACKNOWLEDGEMENTS

I would like to thank first, my family, especially Sue, for supporting me in the research and writing of all the work on the last days. Their practical approach and curiosity kept me level- headed in a subject for research which has many deep ends to fall off. The fact that the material has many practical applications in our own walk and in evangelism has also given a clear focus.

I am, of course, indebted to all my teachers and colleagues and students over the years who have sharpened my skills and perceptions. The staff at Wipf & Stock have also been most helpful and supportive.

Contrary to what some might expect, I have been little influenced by the popular literature, such as Hal Lindsey's work, or the *Left Behind* series of books. In fact, I did not consult such works until after I had finished writing and researching, and found that they had little to add and often seemed to conflate events and ideas that are clearly separate in Scripture. Nonetheless, the popular literature on this topic certainly has its place, maintaining a lively interest in a biblical subject which permeates the whole of Scripture. I am at least indirectly indebted to all such who have gone before. The gospel cannot live without a biblical hope for the future.

PROLOGUE

c. 2082 AD, c. Millennium (Mill.) 40

Paul Christopher, formerly Saul Davidsen, lives as a fully redeemed and regenerated saint during the millennial reign of Christ, about 40 years into the millennium. He is asked to look back and review his journey for a young man and his wife, Jonathan and Sarah, mortals born c. 2054 (Mill. 12) to earth-dwellers who survived Armageddon. They married in 2080. They are struggling with their faith and how there can be two different types of humans alive on earth, immortals like Paul and mortals like themselves.

Paul tells them the story of his life's journey into eternal life to give them hope and to help them realize that they cannot become immortal by any means of their own. Their questions and responses become more and more faithful throughout the story.

We, Jonathan and Sarah, came together
in conviction of our deep abiding need,
not for each other—
our love is deep and true—
but for the knowledge, faith and love
of Him who rules the world,
in the world, not from above,
who has done so openly for 100 years,
since the great destruction of the tribulation wars.

Our parents, children of unbelieving earth-dwellers,
somehow survived and, in repentance, thrived
when the dark veil disappeared,
in the light of Him who cast down all their fears,
destroying Antichrist and his deceptions.

And we, brought up in fear of the Lord,
saw all his marvelous works unfold,

the transformation and restoration of the world.
Who would have thought
such great destruction could be repaired,
yet in decades the world flowered again,
as the human race under divine reign
saw progress, happiness and redemption.

Yet a shadow lay on many a mind,
of those who survived the judgments three:
though no demon could affect our mortal kind,
sin still had a place, a silent, waiting enemy.
One fell thought persisted in many a heart,
envy and jealousy of those who were set apart,
one of whom was Paul, our friend.
Such feelings were kept in check but passed on
to each generation in the millennium,
to bear bitter fruit at the Great White Throne.

And we, Jon and Sarah, had no exemption
from such temptation; Paul and his like
seemed privileged beyond our comprehension.
No sickness or suffering seemed to touch them,
the One always there to save,
strength of mind and body well beyond our own,
they live on, young of heart and soul,
immortal flesh and bone,
while our generations pass mortal to the grave.

But in the midst of all our doubts and fear,
in fact, at their height,
Paul one day appeared,
knew presciently our moral plight,
offered help to dispel what we feared.
And fear we did, that we
could never pass the test.
Sin was always knocking at our door,

though life was good and full and beautiful,
our hearts could have no rest.
"Dear Paul," we said, for he was our friend,
assisted in our needs, and they were many,
"when we compare ourselves to your kind,
we lose hope,
that we can approach our savior worthy.
Please help us to understand
and not despair,
we know that is a path
into the devil's snare."

With grace and a friend's smile he sat down,
to tell us the story of his life,
a life of struggle and determination,
misdirected, over-compensated,
full of strife,
shadows which had far surpassed our own,
dark associations,
but light which broke through,
to bring him to this place.
He spoke as though the memories were fresh and new,
always present, painful too,
yet swallowed up in peace, life and grace.

And Paul began his story . . .

1 THE BEGINNING

2013 AD

Our reluctant hero, Saul Davidsen, age 33, has a vision one morning while walking home from a long night out. He tries to suppress it, but the starkness of its imagery continues to recur.

My name was Saul,
after a maternal grandfather,
and a favorite author
of tales of woe and hope,
something of a secular seer.

This, my tale of woe and hope,
begins with an act of grace.
Yet only God, as I have discovered since,
is gracious, His word alone is true.
I had lived
too long hidden in shadow,
a loveless game player,
projecting my false image,
my lost soul shrouding my vision,
yet vainly imagining I, poor, overeducated, unredeemed fool,
could deliver the world from confusion.

And so I was, body and mind exhausted,
walking the long journey home
early in the morning.
As Helios came up in rose-tinted aurora,
something intervened, in full radiance of light from light together,
made the glorious dawn look like a daub in dried blood;
I saw a being of light descending,
his vast trumpet voice
(it was a he, I am sure, but ask not how or why)

shattered my preconceptions,
demanding of me:
"Hold each word and vision fast,
and though, for now, you will not understand,
others have the will and purpose to fully comprehend."

Painful it was, yet I saw and heard it all in a moment,
not only my own life flashing before my eyes,
but the world's events unfolding, it seemed a death dream.
Sweet and sour, my mouth delighted to find words to describe it,
but my belly bitter because still inadequate.

Who could convey such a vision, was it real anyway?
Whatever real means?
Or just a flashback to the drug my friends put in the coffee months ago?
The angel, for such he was, Uriel was his name, struck me with a rod of iron
and I fell, insensible, doubting and fearing to doubt,
proved a double-minded fool.

Uriel roared at me,
"Listen! You were born deaf, but open your ears,
hear the word spoken in golden prophecy,
things that have been, are, and will be.
God is the door, open the Word and read His silver poesy.
Some people's words and knowledge may open doors,
but His mysteries contain wisdom and understanding,
wisely giving and withholding access,
as your feeble condition demands.
If anointed, poor, unworthy, you may discern the words,
gifted from God's gracious throne.

"Because,
In the beginning, in the beginning was the Logos,
light was, and darkness twisted from it.

Bearer of light became visible darkness,
trying to bend all to his dark will,
and you, O foolish twisted ones, followed,
half-heartedly, whimpering to your death,
hating, embracing the bloody scythe,
outside a lost home of hope you writhe.
But darkness will finally be untwisted,
and His light in you will shine,
resting in His and your eternal dominion."

What could I say or do?
Knowing little of angels and less of God, never read the Book,
but knew some quotes from Muslim and atheist evangelists,
a use for a different purpose.
Why me? It made no sense,
I lived only in the present tense,
past gone and useless,
the future realm the home of Nostradamus.
Ha ha, soon I would forget this hallucination,
my rational mind consigned it to oblivion.

2 BIRTH PAINS

c. 2020–2023 AD

In the following years Saul starts to wonder about the unusual events going on in the world, and he also encounters a clear exposition of the gospel for the first time, though he is at a loss to understand it.

The years went by and I perceived,
that something wicked this way walked,
then as it seemed it ran full pace,
until *pan-demonium* was full on,
in my face.
Irrational wars, needless famine in more than food,
natural disasters and diseases which seemed to have
more than natural consequences.
There was no hiding, the neurotic world I hated,
was now in a psychosis, hunting the sane,
no refuge to be found except in base compliance.

At least so I thought and so complied,
but many were held up to scorn, unjustly tried,
in a court with no law, no rules, no rational guide,
by self-appointed judges, in anonymity,
their votes decided the description of reality,
to destroy the real lives of those who disagree.

But social madness was not the only sign,
that troubled my already troubled mind.
I could hardly talk to any man, woman or child,
without detecting deception in their speech,
their mind, their ratiocinations wild.
And those who gave us all the facts, (the need-to-know ones),
all checked, approved, hyper collaborative,
often reeked of deception, of themselves and of us.

What trust could I give, yet I could hardly disagree,
their narrative so reasonable, even expressed spiritually.

And so, my spiritual search began, birthed in the confusion
of a very modern man.
My questions were quite shallow, why was my world upending?
Even the things I thought were good and so postmodern,
coming back to bite me.
The good of those who ruled the roost
annoyed the remnant of my reason,
and I could not shake the vivid fact of my experience of the vision.
History showed huge varieties of spiritual experience,
good, bad, and indifferent, who was to say?
I would not and could not,
though sensing that the planted seed was coming to fruition.
Ready or not, I felt it, the invader,
yet continued to resist,
that fruit might prove too bitter.

To ease the nagging pain, I plunged into what I knew:
arduous study, history of religions,
geopolitics, anthropology, philosophy,
yet they were changing too.
Would they mean anything,
in the society of the few,
who from their rich enclave,
dispensed the ministry of truth?

Daring not to speak my doubts,
to risk the clamor of their vigorous shouts,
with none to share, to care, in solitude
I reached the end of my ability,
to reconstruct reality in a form I could endure.
The shallow questions left behind,
the voice of Uriel came to mind,

"Do not seek things for yourself, seek Him who sent me."
The floodgates opened a little and I knew,
despite my indoctrination, that I was something special,
beyond the platitudes of modern education.

The question now depended on acceptance of the vision,
if it was real and my perception true,
I should have a sense of mission.
Yet here I was, as far as I knew,
woefully inadequate, uninformed, unreligious,
in a word ignorant, of every single aspect
of this revelation.
The cry of my heart went out to I knew not what,
"Teach me, help me to know my way,
through this bog of a world,
to find firm ground to live on."

Inadequate, self-centered, but enough,
to start the wheels of heaven turning.

And they did not turn slowly, as the old saying goes,
yet my turn would seem slowest, my shameful choices.

That very night as I sat watching in the park,
a sunset in cloudy radiance and color deep and red,
a man who seemed familiar came and sat with me.
Nonetheless I said straight up,
"You may, of course, share the bench with me,
but I am in no mood for talk, please respect my frailty."
He replied, completely disregarding,
"How could you not want to share,
this beauty set before you?
Is your heart in such pain
that this glory comes between us?"

I knew right then, this was no chance,
and the true glory and beauty he referred,
was that of his vision and mine;
yet I sensed,
to his understanding I would defer.
No words came to my lips,
yet he answered my soul's cry,
said, "You have had a vision of the Lord of light, yes?"
I could only nod in reply.
"Do you know the source of what you saw?
Until you grasp that, the meaning will be elusive."
This one clearly was no judge at law,
so I opened my mouth and said, "Friend,
tell me then, because I am at a loss,
to understand and know how this unreal can mend
my unreality to be less meaningless."

Without hesitation he replied,
"The one who showed you what is coming to pass,
placed a seed inside your troubled heart,
not in the vision alone,
but in the circumstances of your childhood life."
I knew at once what that could mean,
but was his knowledge at an end,
the product of trained mind or educated guess work?
He continued, "When you sat near the ocean,
all seven years old upon that rock,
warmed by the sun during a happy day,
watching a glorious sunset much like this,
did you not know with quiet certainty that He exists?"

"It's true," I replied, "but I had nearly forgotten that sweet hour.
Yet though I now recall and feel the joy once more,
how does this help me find the way?"
Again, his reply came instantly,
"He is the way, He is the truth,

He is the life you seek,
seek only Him and you will find the path."
A cloud shaded my heart and I responded,
"My studies show me where this saying comes from:
it comes from the Nazarene,
he who claimed to be God himself.
My mother Miriam, was an unobservant Jew,
with a liberal heritage;
my father Johan an atheist
from a line of Danish atheists,
my doubts are deeply rooted.
If God exists can a man be God,
and how can his claims be verified?"

He paused, as if listening to another voice,
then spoke with clear conviction:
"We all have stumbling blocks,
yet yours are but small stones.
Consider not what your parents were,
but what they have become.
Though you have not seen them for many years,
their course is nearly run.
Speak to them and speak to God,
before they pass in tears,
for the fate of their son."
Rising, he spoke once more,
"The Spirit sends me now from here,
to speak to other souls in need;
go right now to find reconciliation there,
give and find peace of mind
for you and your parents' hearts."

Yet I did not go straightaway,
I had parted from them in acrimony,
when they had found, what I considered,
a false spirituality.

They had indeed found Jesus,
as they said it,
but I was too hardheaded to receive,
so I fled it.
Estranged we were,
but now some common ground had appeared.

3 A DIFFICULT LABOR

c. 2023–2025 AD

Saul puts off going to see his parents, though he senses some urgency, but then the world takes a large turn for the worse and he visits them. They try to explain their walk with Jesus/Yeshua to him and what they understand of the gospel, but he falls back on his barely comprehended Jewish heritage as a means of escape.

His parents, both born in 1955, 1970s' teens who had Saul in 1980 when they were 25, become involved deeply in an alternative economy and lifestyle, preparing the way for those who will be left behind in the rapture event they are convinced will happen soon. They become hard to contact. Soon they will disappear altogether in mysterious circumstances.

Although I saw some common ground for meeting,
still felt the shame of our sad separation,
yet anger too because of their insisting,
on something I could only see
as reason's abdication.

I fell back to my work,
solving problems with computing;
AI was now my friend,
and they offered me promotion.

So, I drifted, work-bound,
a year or more,
but the vision would recur.
The image of my parents did not fade,
and the times became hard to endure,
all pervading fear.
Mugged several times and no one cared,
filth on the streets that no one cleaned,

religious and political wars out there,
to the death,
the nuclear threat hanging over all,
false fears generated by profiteers,
all longing for a leader who would care,
till I, angry and in despair,
committed to find some resolution,
obeying the call of family and tradition.

I stood upon their doorstep,
preparing arguments in my head,
but longing for them in my heart.
Why was there a mezuzah on the post?

The door opened,
my mother Miriam laughed,
my father, Joe, ran to meet me.
I could but mutter, welcomed in,
hugged like a long-lost friend.
My heart was touched but head overruled,
and all I could do was question,
though some would call it interrogation.

"Yes, good to see you, but,
I have come for understanding.
Understand that I still cannot
reconcile the message you are preaching.
Why a mezuzah at your door?
I know it's a very Jewish thing,
but, Mother, you forsook the Jewish life,
adapted to a life of anathema;
I am no Jew but this takes some explaining.
Does it not contain a prayer,
which sums up all that old dogma?"

Between them both, in intimate collusion,
they showed me why, in their faithful minds,
there was no obscure confusion.
"You are not entirely right, but who can blame,
we erred because of the godless way we raised you.
Forgive us Son, but there is a greater reason,
the mezuzah is only one expression
of a profound and penetrating truth
which, irrevocably, has changed us both.

"But let us start from that simple thing:
the mezuzah is a teaching object,
it will serve to lead us to the depth,
for which your heart is longing.

"The doorpost is a significant icon,
in the ancient Jewish tradition,
for keeping evil out and holiness in.
The message contained,
in that little space,
is full of life and grace,
a covenant with God.
Love Him with all your being,
and show it in your life,
bring down His blessing,
and the latter rain.
You could not know this, yet you feel it,
unwilling to be deceived and follow evil masters,
and despite our remissness,
your soul longs for completion,
in the faith of our fathers,
not least great Abraham.

"Will you hear us now, curb your fear,
though poor, blind and foolish we have been,
explain the truth which led us here,
yet still connected to the great tradition?"

I nodded, "Please, go on, I will be mute."
Could their resolution be justifiable,
of that which to me so irresolute,
seemed irreconcilable?
(I knew that I knew nothing,
yet hubris raised its head still).
"The mezuzah texts have their counterpart,
fulfillment of the covenant,
in the prophet's words in our Tanach.
Not least in Isaiah's noble One,
who brings salvation to us, Zion,
He who suffered the curse for us upon a tree,
in chapters fifty-two and fifty-three,
for so those accursed do die,
though He for you and me."

They read the texts to me right then,
and I thought I felt approaching dawn
yet, just before the light broke in,
I broke out with a yawn,
a mist descending on my brain,
a veil fell over my tired eyes.
I could not, would not comprehend,
yet their hope and faith
could not be disparaged.
A different path I must follow soon,
to discover my Jewish heritage.

I took my leave, expecting disappointment,
but they, in all gracious calm,
accepted my decision,
though parting with a Parthian shot,
trusting God to guide the shaft.
"We may not see you ever again,
the times have become much harsher;
if not, remember our love for you,

and know that God loves you better.
He will guide you in the way,
until at last we come together."
They were right about the times,
we kept in touch by email, spasmodically,
but then the flow dried up, dramatically.
Looking back, I realized that they had chosen,
to walk the path off-grid,
and though they had no survivalist vision,
teaching others how to survive hell on earth
was the center of their mission.
And though I thought their labor was a waste,
I understood their heart was for others;
they worked not for their own preservation,
the bottom line was,
they trusted God's salvation.

It seemed a flashback to the seventies,
when the hippies that they were
established cooperatives,
to share and care for the poor and each other.
Yet now the stakes were higher,
for many it would mean life or death.

Because of our former bitter separation,
none associated me with their work;
but conversations overheard soon revealed
that if I was linked with their mission,
I would be branded by association,
an outcast from even my limited inner circle,
and soon enough out of work.
Anger and fear filled my heart,
at the fate I saw encroaching on our lives,
and theirs particularly when they achieved
a measure of local fame, for helping
those who could not help themselves.

And yet because they took the faithful stand,
exploited and harassed as terrorists,
undermining the emergent dark consensus,
of what it meant to be a human person.
My work enabled me to slip between the cracks,
of a world cracking up on specious facts,
and there were many.
Yet I feared those my parents would offend,
knew the power that could be exercised,
if they chose to silence those who turned
against the thought miasma of the day.

The time came soon enough,
a phone call from my mother,
of all things from a burner phone she said,
certain they were being followed and surveilled.
Black cars, black threats, made anonymously,
the self-appointed delatores[1] made free,
to ruin their lives and destroy the work,
unwittingly refining their profound intention,
to set others free from such domination.
Her spirits high she said, "We love you",
Joe echoing her sentiment.
They did not press me on my spiritual walk,
their destiny was secure but mine still in the air.
We parted on good terms,
they in hope and me still garbed in fear.
And then it all went dark, no word,
they just went missing and the authorities presumed
they had joined the ranks of the homeless on the street,
and perished as so many do,
anonymous, forsaken, yet they knew,
their Savior they would meet.

1. Delator: an old Roman word for an informant who handed over criminals (often political outcasts) in the expectation of reward, then a quarter of the betrayed person's property. However, if the person proved innocent of the charges, the delator received the punishment intended for the person falsely accused.

4 HEAVEN'S DECREE

c. 2026 AD

While struggling to come to terms with his Jewish heritage, the loss of his parents and what they had told him, Saul meets and is deceived by an antichrist/false prophet, who plays on his Jewish heritage and twists what his parents told him about Jesus as Messiah to confuse him.

Uriel appears to Saul again. He takes Saul into the heavens to witness the heavenly court and the judgments of Revelation 4 and 5. Saul is overwhelmed and realizes that the supreme figure is the Messiah, but his experience with the false prophet blocks his recognizing the Messiah as Yeshua. Various signs indicate that a breakpoint is coming.

In limbo I remained for many a month,
covertly pursuing my parents' fate,
yet filled with hopelessness; there was no debate
as to what was coming soon upon this planet.
Sensed a dark barbarian fatalism, nihilistic tyranny,
of those who hate kings and queens, trolls
who yet lust for empire in their small worlds,
a world of individuals craving order and control,
but only on their own terms,
and so,
inevitably,
preparing the way for a Brobdingnagian doom.

At last I mourned my parents.
They were gone,
as I would be soon if my secret thoughts were known,
and yet one day I awoke to see,
a new dawn, a bright and cheerful light,
breaking in on me.
Unaccountably refreshed in spirit,
I took a day off from my trade,

(working flexible hours, they did not pay as much).
As I walked the sun warmed my face.
Closed eyes, open mind I walked a side path blind,
opened them to see a man block my way,
his face concerned and benign.
"Are you well, young man?" he asked,
his tone mellifluous, filled with intelligent respect.
"Yes, sir," I replied, "thank you for your concern,
yet I often walk like this, to ease my troublesome care,
a certain peace I gain, when I simply trust my feet."
"Ah well," said he, "there's something to be said for that,
but in this bright sun should you not have a hat?"
He clearly shared the common bane,
fearing skin cancer and all its promised pain.
So though I judged his zeal misjudged,
from one barely older than me,
we continued conversationally
his voice resounding pleasantly.

Unwise perhaps, I shared my present loss,
and even some superficial, noncommittal thoughts
(or so I reasoned)
on the state of the dominion.
In smooth and friendly words,
he soothed my hesitant fears,
inquired gently after my opinion,
on the nature of philosophy and religion,
and my heritage in those domains.
He seemed to sense, or, even know,
the struggles I had been through,
my parents' faith, of which, oddly,
I spoke to him only in the negative.
Aroused, my innate curiosity,
when it was his turn to speak,
I listened close and eagerly.

"Young man," he said, (though young he seemed),
"I sympathize, share some Jewish blood" (he lied).
"I have seen these struggles often,
among my peers and the younger generation.
The struggle has persisted for 2,000 years,
yet all such problems have a ready solution.
The crux of the matter, who is the Messiah?
The problem solved in your heart,
release all your desire.
Realize your full potential, as I have realized mine,
I am he and you can be too,
an unequivocally anointed one.
You could worship the messiah in me,
and I in you,
though little revealed yet
in your unenlightened state.
You, a lesser emanation may, one day,
approach my exaltation.

"Your mother and father chose the hard way,
an unnecessary path, and though
we should not deny their sincere intent,
sincerity may not be correct.
The law and prophets are very clear,
the Messiah must come in glory,
to cast down every enemy
and exalt all his chosen ones,
and how could he not come,
except in the heart of all his Jewish people?

"When we rise up, we will overcome,
to destroy all god-hating Gentiles.
Your mother and father were too literal,
God, the Messiah, they thought,
was a person, yet by definition
he can only be a spirit.

Do not even the Christians say,
his spirit dwells within them,
and did not the prophet Jesus say through Luke,
the kingdom of God is within you?
Would not the mutual worship of messiah
in one another, the essence of the law fulfill,
love your neighbor as yourself.
And if one should arise fully realized,
as Messiah King"
(he meant himself, of course)
"could we not all worship him?"

Was it the argument, or the words
so soothingly delivered,
my troubled mind found rest,
though a nagging doubt persisted.
Clearly this worshipful wise man knew more than me,
but that was nothing,
since nothing effectual had I learned of the tradition.

We talked on late into the afternoon,
he opened vistas theological and political,
all tending, I noticed in retrospect,
to exalt his own opinion and interpretation.
He claimed that we, or was it only he?
could make miracles happen.
Yet such was the power of his person,
I could not allow myself any animosity.

But I grew tired and the day grew long,
so when he sensed my wearied acquiescence,
took his leave with a promise to return,
to finish our enlightened conversation.

Away from his presence, my mind began to reclaim,
contradictions that my parents had already given,

and so the seed of doubt was sown,
would the harvest be the same?

That night I lay upon my bed,
no rest for this mind ill-led,
filled with contradictions.
Suddenly, I yielded to a cowardly prompting,
or so my adverse mind described it,
asked God to show me who He was,
to resolve the twisted Gordian knot,
whose strands threefold ran twined through
my body, soul and spirit.

The answer came like a thunderclap,
with lightning everywhere.
In my dreams or in a vision,
was I earthbound or in heaven?
I know not, God knows.
Barely had I closed my eyes than my other eyes were open,
and Uriel my friend appeared again, to lead me into wonders
I never could imagine.
Beings of light permeated by a greater light,
full of power and the perfect fear of God,
even the physical objects exquisite beyond compare.
Yet all this glory to a singular end,
on this occasion,
destruction of that ancient predatory fiend.
In all that awesome beauty,
a court decision, final judgment,
of just and holy war ultimate.
And at the center a Lamb,
like none I had ever seen.
Somehow, I knew he was the essence,
of God, Messiah, King of kings,
to whom belongs all praise.

A Lamb worthy to open the judgment scroll,
indictment, charge and sentence inevitable,
on all his reckless foes.
None else in heaven nor below on earth,
could pay the heavenly price,
to stand in our place.
Thank God that only his Messiah reveals
what's been concealed since creation's birth.
Emerald rainbow, bloodstones and thrones,
thunder, lightning, seven fiery lamps.
Elders twenty-four cast down their crowns,
for he alone is worthy of all praise,
to open the scroll and loose its holy seals.

The prayers of the saints rise as incense,
elders and angels praise the Great Redeemer,
everything in heaven and on earth gives voice.
So, you, fall down and worship him forever,
for worthy is the Lamb who was slain,
in his high kingdom neither death nor pain.
All is ready, the great finale will soon begin,
few the elect though great in number
living and dead soon rise in hidden rapture.

I fell down on my knees as one dead,
but Uriel bent down to raise my head:
"Remember what you have seen,
and come soon to a decision,
the day is drawing near,
for salvation or condemnation."

I fell into the deepest sleep,
awoken by the morning sun,
I had forgotten nothing,
the whole vision returning,
sharp and clear.

Yet I was filled with fear,
not because the meaning was opaque,
judgment was inevitable,
but who was the Lamb?
Though he must be the Messiah,
what did it mean that he was slain?
The conflict within me rose again,
I remembered the words of the worldly wiseman
(though wise now he seemed not,
in the light of true Messiah)
and though I knew his story full of errors,
I failed to sort the wheat from the tares.

I understood now what the angel said,
a choice must be made:
Who is the Messiah that I have seen?
Why was the Lamb slain?
What does it mean,
for salvation and condemnation,
most especially mine?

Yet one choice I irrevocably made,
The lamb, the Messiah, I had seen was a Jew,
and my Jewish heritage could no longer be suppressed,
my inheritance that of Israel, my aim to renew
connection with the faith my family had rejected.

5 HIDDEN RAPTURE

c. 2027 AD

Saul weighs the evidence from his parents, the Jewish Bible and the false prophet and what Uriel has shown him, but is left in limbo about Yeshua's identity and significance.
The hidden rapture occurs and Saul has to come to terms with it.

He concludes that he has to gather and weigh up more evidence, including the evidence from the New Testament.

My father and mother had told me many things,
and asked me to accept them at face value,
their meaning to be revealed by life's events,
prophecy of the moment understood, retrospectively.

As Enoch and Elijah ascended, so would every believer,
and this would be a sign, the beginning of the end.
And the end will be full of terror,
for as Antiochus Epiphanes slew the faithful Jews,
desecrated their temple,
so would one arise to destroy Christian churches
and Jacob's believing people.
A new temple will become his seat, of power and deception,
at first peaceful and benevolent,
but bent on bloody insurrection.
Many troubles, plagues, wars and great disasters
would come upon a world bereft of understanding.
Babylon would rise again and open Ishtar's gate,
perpetrating a holocaust of Jew and Gentile who resist,
put to shame the guillotine of the 1790s,
and all in God's holy name, in global slaughters.
And yet, they also said,
judgments would rebuke Babel's fearsome rage,
yet never satisfied she,

nor the bloodlust of her acolytes,
and close to the end she herself will be destroyed,
her beastly use expired.

Though much of what they said
overlapped with my dreams,
it was too much for me, to absorb or comprehend,
my vision too obscured to believe,
that such things could come to be,
surely, they were but fantasy,
explained well enough by Fraser's *Golden Bough.*
How could another temple come to be? World War Three
would surely eventuate,
and though Israel was once more a powerful state,
the Jewish people would never take the risk.
And all this talk of holocausts,
of Christians and of Jews,
was insensitive to say the least
in the struggle against the anti-Semites.

So, the veil remained over my eyes,
though some holes had been poked in it,
and the backburner seemed the place to put,
all those fearful end-times' expectations.

The days wore on, the world came bleaker,
successfully I hid my perturbations,
from my bosses and my friends,
afraid of being seen as a right-winger.

Often walking in the park and along the beaches,
I stood at a distance, distantiated
from the many independent preachers,
whose urgent messages surged over,
my saturated yet resistant mind.

Almost as one, their message seemed to match
the elements of my visions, and
my parents' fervent mission.
A kaleidoscope of passions:
anger, fear, renewed love for father and mother,
a hopeful spirit gnawing at the foundation,
of my intellectual aspiration.

And then it happened.

Sunset again, in the park, walking among the flower beds,
lit up in preternatural light,
I spied my evangelist talking to another soul,
on the same park bench where he spoke to my spirit.
Several soap-box preachers were also within hearing,
I looked at them directly,
and then they were not,
their bodies simply,
disappearing.
And not just them, but several others faded,
became holes in the crowd which went unnoticed,
except within the field of my vision.
I glanced to see my evangelist, but he was gone as well,
the woman he had been talking to,
jumping up and away,
hands to her mouth, face pale with fear,
screaming to no one in particular,
she ran as though the hounds of hell came after.

Then many started running,
who did not turn first to their dead devices,
and all were moving,
a heaving, rushing chaos,
even those who had not seen,
swept up in mad panic,
desperate for news of those they loved

and hoped were still living.
Of how and why,
what did it mean,
they collided with each other,
a world in collision and confusion.

And here and there, in fact everywhere,
howls of horror and loss.
Yet eclipsing them all,
a distraught, keening wail,
the dread and helpless terror of those who knew,
they had been left behind,
resonating dully in my own shocked heart,
not knowing yet its full meaning,
or even my own mind.

It took but moments until I woke,
in bitter shock and partial understanding,
looked up to see what could be,
but no fiery chariot,
no angelic trumpeting,
they were simply gone,
and I knew,
we now faced a great accounting.

What must I do?
My parents' warning words contained a hint of salvation,
possible even after the great translation.
God, I knew, existed,
but the devils know that is true,
and because the Spirit was not within me
still thought knowledge was the key.
I had not known His perfect time,
unlike my parents,
I unholy, unfaithful, vacillating,
had imagined kinship with the Lord

though unbelieving.
So, he came when I was all unready,
to escape what came to pass, unworthy.

Unworthy as I had been to hear
the trumpet blast which took them in the air,
for reports of those who saw them directly
said that each of the taken looked up suddenly
cried out something like, "The trumpet sounds!"
Then they were gone.

Clearly, my parents could be right and I wrong,
about Messiah's true identity.
They had known much more than me,
integrated their lives with future history,
therefore, I had to relearn
the lessons of life and philosophy,
applied to the religion I thought they owned.
Yet the Spirit still prompted me,
buried deep within my soul,
a half-formed seed planted,
sensed that knowledge could not set me free,
unless my mind be opened,
to wisdom from a place more holy.

I had not the courage, nor wealth,
(the state had confiscated all my parents owned),
to dive into the foreign world,
forbidden and forbidding,
of yeshiva or seminary,
but effectively online pursued their deep study
of the Book and all its implications.
Always good at languages
soon learned enough of ancient Hebrew,
koine Greek, Aramaic and Arabic,
and expanded the little Latin that I knew.

Between Chabad and Christian extremity,
from Rav Ketina to Hal Lindsey,
soon learned enough to confuse the sharpest mind,
especially since I had to balance the new insights
with the intrusive, antithetic demands
of social and workplace protocols.

Yet learn I did and began to understand at last,
something deeper must happen,
a transformation of the heart.

6 THE VIOLENT PRELUDE TO PEACE

c. 2027–2030 AD

The world reacts badly to the sudden loss of millions of people, blaming each other and descending for a time into anarchy and civil war in many places. Saul is relatively insulated from the worst of it but has his own internal war to deal with.

Saul commits to a full-time course of study of the New Testament particularly, when a fortuitous transfer opportunity to Jerusalem comes up courtesy of the antichrist/false prophet whom he meets once more, though now Saul is mysteriously protected from his deception and discernment.

In the course of this decision-making, he is constantly confronted by the consequences of the loss of so many true Christians, (yet the retention of so many professing Christians, often of high rank in the church), but is unsure about the Antichrist who appears on the world scene, and who seems to be doing good things like rebuilding the Jewish temple, making world peace etc. The Antichrist's wars before the peace raise up 10 leaders who control the armies in 10 significant world locations and act as military governors. But he also begins to build up systems of social credit and personal identification preceding what will become the mark of the beast. The New Babylon, under the False Prophet begins to emerge after the wars which destroyed many of the old commercial centers.

The Antichrist's political seat of world government is in Jerusalem while the False Prophet confirms a world religious and cultural system based in Babylon, called New Babylon. The seven Babylonian world centers begin to usurp some or much of the political control the 10 military leaders first exercised.

These world centers will have a cultural and religious focus, particularly to assist the apprehension of 'terrorists' who want to limit the new leader's power and return to a democracy dimly remembered. Some tension has been created within his global empire by the replacement of the ten 'kings' with seven rulers of the Babylon system that the False Prophet sets up, and signs of this start to emerge.

6 The Violent Prelude to Peace

The Minor Tribulation

I, less confused than many,
but most of the world had nothing
like the benefit of my conditioning,
my parents' lessons now engraved,
in my mind,
if still not in spirit fully understood.

And the world reacted badly:
defense systems, keyed to AI,
assumed the loss of population
to be the consequence of enemy action.

North Korea reacted first:
losing full 10 percent of their population,
unexpected, and surprising so many,
yet gone they were, all of faith . . .
there could only be one material explanation!
They had been renditioned to the south,
defectors all, but the property of Kim,
the US imperialists were to blame.
Almost without thought,
reactionary, the missiles flew to Seoul
and US military bases.
Even from two subs small tactical nukes
fell on Los Angeles and New York,
no warning calls,
Manhattan and Hollywood gone,
and a million souls,
the rest in agony from radiation.
Almost instantly, within the day,
North Korea vanished from the map,
in angry retaliation.

Yet Korea not the worst or greatest,
almost a footnote,
to the wars unleashed,
throughout the Middle East.
As many vanished throughout Iran,
Egypt, Iraq, Syria and Afghanistan,
not to mention Israel,
the hidden faithful gone,
their inexplicable loss a flail,
in every nation
scoring open wounds
of ancient provenance.

Opportunistically,
many tried to destroy the Jewish state,
(as well as each other);
heavy missiles by the dozen
through the Iron Dome did penetrate.
Yet hasty vengeance so often bites the biter,
and missiles with bioweapons went astray,
not just to Jewish settlements and cities
the prime targets,
but in Palestinian areas to their dismay.
The guilty would blame Israel
for wholesale genocide,
when they themselves were guilty
of launching mass fratricide.
But Israel could not entirely stop the fiery storm,
they too had lost many,
diminished command and control,
and divided among themselves,
like a dark cloud fell the locust swarm,
missiles with grim names,
major cities suffered a heavy toll.
Even holy Jerusalem struck,

though not quite destroyed,
by the one and only tactical nuke
which penetrated the shield.
Ground zero inadvertently became Al Aqsa,
every building and wall leveled in Old Jerusalem,
the massive ancient foundation stones of the wall
still stood, grim and stark
amidst the smoking rubble.

And many smaller rockets went astray,
a stolen tactical missile stockpile,
a nuclear and biochemical array,
well-hidden for a rainy day,
destroying Jew and Filastin alike,
in every territory death held sway.
And like the USA,
the response was immediate,
with armament more accurate and precise,
Damascus, Baghdad, Tehran, Kabul, Amman
and more, extinguished in a night.
Iran also took out her opposition:
Saudi capital obliterated,
even Mecca and Medina wiped clean,
and so Karbala gone,
as if swept with a broom.
No one knew who launched at them,
nor at Jerusalem, (except the man of sin)
but the geography of faith was purged,
the power of Sunni and Shia all but gone,
and though Israel emerged
more or less intact, by God's protection,
she the only effective power which remained,
the region had become
a blank slate for some new god to write on.

And nations rallied to support,
one side or another
in the struggle which ensued.
The entire Middle East
became the largest battleground
for a proxy World War Three
between the now greatly weakened powers of the world.

For none escaped the terror of civil war,
not so much geographical but more
ideological and emotional division.
So city fought country to destruction,
in many places literally;
the middle class against both rich and poor,
the poor against all, and each other,
wealth destroyed, the rich fewer,
though still in power,
but poverty the victor.

Open were Hell's gates,
Hell's riders riding forth,
bow, sword, famine, plague, wild beasts,
weighed in the balance,
mene, mene, tekel parsin.

And when those greatest killers rose,
famine and pestilence,
they took their toll in every place,
throughout a world in chaos.

The Rise of the Antichrists

But hope emerged out of all this fear,
whispers of one who while unmatched in war,
yet sought reconciliation and true peace,
somehow found food to feed the hungry well,

protected the weak and weary masses
from the depredations of those who still
fanned the flames of ancient hatreds.

I, Saul, safe for now in America,
the nation only lightly touched,
compared to some,
though brutal civil war loomed on the horizon.
I could barely comprehend,
the scale of this destruction,
the lightning speed of the transition
from what seemed the world's normal pattern
to a routine of extreme disruption.

Though many nations were protected
by their relative isolation,
all were brutalized by civil wars;
neighbors and deplorables
of every denomination,
all affected by loss and privation.
The call to war readiness expected
but unreal, all in shock, traumatized,
supply lines broken,
food costs now beyond the means of many.
Those who could have given spiritual food,
were taken.
And America, like all the others, was soon riven,
by civil strife incomprehensible;
no simple North and South division,
but complex battles between and within cities,
often at the same time, irreconcilable,
rural heartland against the urban coasts,
neighbors at war with each other.

I could not change the world,
but I was another matter.

Resolved to understand,
suppress the negative chatter
of a mind going quite neurotic,
to form a coherent hermeneutic,
consistent with all
that I had seen and learned,
to build a valid view of the world
and its real meaning understand.
I committed to more study, thought and meditation,
trying to resolve the tension threatening us,
how to reconcile all this suffering and pain,
with my parents' God of peace and grace.

Yet if I seemed interested in such things,
seeking spiritual truth even to a small degree,
apart from the now politically correct social focus,
inclined towards the value of tradition,
my social life, such as it was,
my hard-won career, fragile prize,
would be damned to perdition.

However, opportunity arose which kept me hidden,
strange as it seemed.
Though infrastructure systems were quite broken,
demand for my IT skills
and AI knowledge had increased,
beyond reason or expectation.
I did not question why,
just glad to have some security,
in a particularly insecure society.

In that comfort zone,
my hopes could still play out,
to understand what was going on,
to investigate and learn, not shout,
against the dreadful fate coming down.

Barely before I could even try to plan
devious diversions of my time,
to suit my covert new goals,
a strange encounter reset my life's direction,
to walk in paths that led
to unexpected illumination.

Once more I encountered my worldly-wise man,
though now I knew he was much more than that;
he sought me out at the place I worked,
in the middle of a crisis, he appeared.
Top management already knew him,
and deferred straightaway when he appeared.
He greeted me as though I was a disciple,
at which they acknowledged me
as a preferential friend.

I thought he would soon see right through me,
as I had seen clear through his smooth seduction,
but though his veil over me was ripped and torn,
there seemed a veil on my behalf
fully over his perception.

"Let me confide in you, my friend,"
he said,
(though friends did not exist in his true dimension).
"This disappearance of so many, better called abduction,
and the resulting war, famine and plague have thrown
the world into consternation.
The turmoil in every heart may soon,
break out in global rebellion,
false hopes and sedition,
and soon I will be called
to a much higher vocation.
Our master will make his seat of power
in Jerusalem, in accord with ancient prophecy,

for despair is come on this old earth,
and from that center planetary,
we will work its resurrection.

"You I call to carry out my express purpose,
as manager of my IT and AI concerns,
restoring good government and peace,
in a world without a benevolent focus."

Clearly, I had been groomed for the task,
in more ways than one;
unseen forces were at work,
not only the will of false prophets,
it all seemed to fit my new intention.
Of course, I acquiesced,
at this great opportunity,
to both make progress in the world,
and fulfill my perceived new destiny.

Little did I realize,
the dangers I would face,
but surfed the wave of fate's designs,
dimly aware of sharp coral reefs.

In the days and weeks that followed
I perceived the scale
of the psychosis he had predicted.
My personal world had suffered little loss,
few in my circle had disappeared,
in social life or workplace.

Yet, for many there had been grievous loss,
whole families gone from their extended family,
young children taken, though often not their parents,
the old left to care for the young untimely,
young men and girls without support suddenly,

explanations nearly as voluminous,
as recriminations.
Systems of health and education faltered,
(the best had often been taken in the disappearing);
unseen till then disease and plagues untreated
took many of the living,
civil strife and lawlessness, governments stumbled
and criminals took leadership from them,
all to their advantage in the moral vacuum.

Through it all the rumor of hope spreading,
a great leader on the horizon,
some fast dismissed such a perfect man
as the product of wishful thinking,
others quick to believe again.

Three trends emerged within a year or so,
and all had an echo in my heart, for good or ill,
one yet another bitter pill but two offered hope,
out of chaos fate entwined them all.
From economic downfall and bitter loss,
a new coinage slowly emerged from the dross,
the value of people, not land or thing,
their social credit moral worth defining.

A new political wave in a new geographical,
shifted the world's power equilibrium,
the old-world centers embroiled in wars uncivil,
power focused in a middle-earth fulcrum,
the geopolitics of
the New Babylon and a new Jerusalem.

The bitter pill: prospect of tyranny
emerged with our new leader,
(though no one seemed aware),
one who defeated the worst of evil easily,

beaten very rarely.
Even in some minor defeat, still ultimately overcame
the gangs, corrupt and desperate former politicians
clinging to their power with main force.
Many rallied to his name,
desperate for order, at any cost,
yet he seemed diffident of fame,
rejecting power absolute.
The masses spoke of him in hope,
yet my heart bade me wait,
and see just how this seeming force for light,
would handle authority so easily bestowed.
Very like he seemed
to the false prophet who conscripted me;
in fact, to him my overseer deferred,
seemed to know him well.
And many lesser such emerged,
with one another all at ease,
though a competitive strain could be discerned,
offering similar remedies, all humanistic,
though some might have said,
subtly demonic.

Ten much like him, but acting more like kings,
emerged as his generals,
ruling all the earth effectively,
from ten regional citadels.
Pacifica, America East and West,
the continent divided vertically;
greater Brazil and Argentina south,
split horizontally, many nations merged,
Africa, West and Eastern Europe,
likewise split all Asia.
The ten ruled with hegemonic power,
power tempered only by the will
of their commander for that hour.

Some of my new Messianic Jewish friends,
who kept a low profile, in a shadow realm,
suggested all were antichrists,
but the Beast greatest of them.
Perhaps they all could have become the one,
but lacked the vision, drive and will to overcome,
and so, one had to emerge, they say,
in whom, soon,
all the power of Hell would display.

Peace and Order Begin to be Restored, c. 2030–2033

As time went on, the Antichrist (to his opposition),
had many reconsidering,
that far from a tyrant in the making,
he might be the healer of a world in desperation.

Put aside his social credit system—
for such would his False Prophet introduce—
excuse the sometimes brutal force
to put down insurrection,
the world wanted order at any price,
and would symbolically at least,
bow the knee to him.

He made his base of power,
in Jerusalem, rebuilt in very short time,
and made another rising star
his cultural adviser, a prophesier,
building a new Babylon.
The great new city of Babel rose from desert sands,
a miracle of technological construction,
created links to the centers of world power,
controlling all through blind devotion,
or forced cooperation, the social credit lever.

His new Jerusalem was the heart political,
of his program of peace,
of all nations the omphalos.
And his gift to the torn nation of Israel,
to seal his power established,
a seven-year treaty of reconciliation
with all her once-were enemies,
the symbol of this unity decreed,
a common new temple on the temple mound,
on the rubble which war created.
Although close examination
revealed a truth profound,
the peace was with and for himself and his own,
his global hegemony, laying the ground,
who could gainsay his victories hard won?
For in the chaos of a collapsing world,
all were desperate to resolve the hatred,
and heal the wounds, bitter rooted,
symbolically seen in the new seat,
of world political power, Zion.
The bait for the Jewish people,
the new temple in a new Jerusalem,
a fit fulfillment of Messianic expectation.

Modelled on Ezekiel's impossible holy place,
the temple rose quickly, beautiful in construction,
with no political opposition,
who was left with power to oppose?
At first the builders went slowly,
aware of Julian's apostate folly,
earthquake and fiery consequences.
But as the structure rose,
beautiful beyond expectation,
the work was soon completed
in hopeful even faithful anticipation.
Inner court and outer court

massive protective walls,
gates at each compass point,
cherubim and palms
carved by true craftsmen on the doors.
The glorious stone which shone like gold
in the rising and setting sun,
precious metals lining the interior,
a river of gold to complete it all,
yet none inquired,
its source in a greatly impoverished world.

Parallel with this, his other great vision,
global culture and economy controlled,
a new world order focused in a new Babylon,
cultural and financial capital of the world.

Jerusalem and Babylon, enemies by tradition,
twin poles for transmission
of compelling power none could resist,
a soft glove covering an iron fist.

7 FIRSTFRUITS

c. 2027–2033 AD

Parallel with the growing influence of the Antichrist and his supporters a powerful, evangelical, Jewish Christian (Messianic) force has been rising. There are 144,000 such witnesses.

The influence of the 144,000 is also evident everywhere, though the mass media try to downplay their existence or even type them as terrorists, undermining the Antichrist's peace. Saul notices that faithful Christians and Jews are being persecuted more, though the Antichrist decries the worst of the apparently random atrocities. Things start to deteriorate and he notices the buildup of troops in Israel and around Jerusalem especially. Various signs indicate that the Antichrist is becoming just that, as he is joined by the False Prophet who encourages adulation of him.

Many, especially the Jewish Christians, try to raise the alarm about the Temple and the Antichrist's intentions. The Jewish Christians leave Jerusalem and Israel en masse. The False Prophet's propaganda prepares the ground of expectation in the earth-dwellers that someone, Christians and Jews inferred, is plotting to overthrow the Antichrist and destroy his peace. The alternative market has become quite strong, especially since the disappearing, and is condemned as undermining the Antichrist's economic reforms, so a new financial loyalty system is mooted and the first steps towards its creation undertaken. This places believers in an invidious situation. They are trying to lay the groundwork to survive an economic system which they know will exclude them but their efforts are being used to justify the introduction of just such a system.

The new temple is also coming to be viewed as a center of insurrection by the Antichrist and his followers. The Antichrist has been introducing new rules allowing himself illegitimate access to the temple, which the Jewish authorities have been resisting. All opposition is portrayed as insurrection.

All this change did not happen overnight,
not without resistance and questioning,
another force for change was working fast,
and had done since the disappearing.
This other power raised its voice,
faith to revive,
with a disturbing counternarrative.

Many were well qualified to tell this story:
those who wailed in disbelief
when friends and relatives were taken into glory,
and they who knew what to expect but left behind,
the faith they had in everything but Christ,
his church, word, message they knew,
but knew not him, their souls tormented.
Determined to discover Him, the Lord, anew,
they would become his true church
to fulfill his mission
in the midst of great tribulation.

From these repentant masses left behind,
New Messianic believers, many a thousand,
took the initiative to lead
the new but bewildered faithful from every faith
against the hierarchy of the apostate.

And although many an old-school liberal stayed cholic,
scoffed at any Bible explanation of the disappearing,
clung desperately to their cosmic christ symbolic,
millions who had not such heavy millstones,
turned to Christ and his word's true meaning.
Revival unparalleled in all the history of the earth,
gave hope and life to many,
though there was a counterstream of death,
of bitter, mostly unspoken enmity.

It seemed the Antichrist gave approval to all faiths,
publicly soliciting hope from people in despair,
in his person seeming hopeful, full of promise,
for a world remade in his design and image fair.

For many his support to build the temple,
validated support for a broad agenda,
to rebuild the world in the image of his maker,
(so he said),
though some concerned
by his growing hold on the mind of the world.

So, against that sovereignty, in that same hour,
arose another, undeclared yet effective power,
many thousands of Jewish evangelists,
speaking out, steeped in law and prophets,
heritage complete in knowledge of Messiah,
drawing millions to the cross of Christ.
Where had they, could they, have come from,
no one knew; even they often knew not
their brothers in the task, each a firstfruit,
yet everyone had a similar story,
had been close to understanding the mystery,
that Christ meant Messiah and Messiah Christ.

The disappearing closed the deal, opened the seal
on their faith, until that moment covered by the veil,
all had seen believers vanish, taken abruptly,
the scales fell from their eyes and they saw instantly,
a complete and informed revelation,
Christ is king over their, and every, nation.

The Antichrist did not move against them then,
even blessing somewhat tepid deigned to give,
decrying attacks on their persons,
yet many attempts were made on their lives,

to no effect, they had divine protection.
This undercurrent of hatred for the faith,
delivered once for all to the saints,
would soon enough break into open persecution,
disguised for the moment, until all was in place.

It was not hard to read, this unsubtle antagonism,
even as in days gone past, media opportunism
portrayed the good as unholy,
the corrupt portrayed contrarily as just and worthy.
Many there were who took the hint, with alacrity,
the Christ-proclaimers were fair game,
their possessions incidental booty.
The victims often portrayed as terrorists,
well deserving of their just rewards.
So Christians forced to meet in private,
few daring public proclamation,
or its likely fate.
The Great Leader, such his lieutenants did proclaim him,
inveighed against the worst attacks,
their seeming randomness sign of the times,
which he could overcome by the power of his name.

And I gave credit where it seemed due: in those times,
wars had ceased, peace established,
though brutally in some cases;
supply lines were restored,
though under martial law and
government controllers.
After only a few unsettled years,
the poor were not poorer,
the rich still happy in their gilded towers.

The new temple was soon built, Jewish and Christian,
even Muslim leaders such as were left,
unified, proclaiming high praise for the Great Leader,

whose vision and wisdom, without doubt,
proclaimed, the person of a Mahdi or Messiah.

And I, Saul, while not entirely taken in,
was part of the rebuilding.
AI used to replace the many missing,
a network of control with little indication,
even I uncertain,
of who was doing the controlling.

As infrastructure rapidly emerged,
in cities sprung from desert sands,
and many overseas,
foundation stones for an empire in the making,
ten centers of regional power created,
in Australasia, the Americas, Europa,
Africa and Asia, each center with a primate city
under a plenipotentiary military governor,
seemed ready to unite in a world authority.

Yet once peace was restored,
a subtle shift of power occurred:
the ten governors of military might,
were sidelined by the False Prophet,
from his base, the Babylonian tower,
seemingly at the behest of the Great Leader.
Territories were merged and consolidated,
a global restructuring,
mere satraps the ten became,
subjects in the False Prophet's jurisdiction,
under seven new rulers he appointed,
himself and his deputy
over three old military sees,
Asian and African,
six others to rule the rest
of the Great Leader's domain,
the world encompassed.

Babylon's voice proclaimed,
a new order was emerging;
soon all would reap the benefit,
of the Great Leader's beneficial planning.
The ways of peace were now in sight,
old martial way was waning.
And though it was evident,
that the old warriors took it bitter,
they ten were still protected,
dark foreboding,
in positions seeming minor.

The trend seemed positive
from a global point of view,
at the local level still misgiving,
for those with eyes to see,
to wonder what else was coming.

I, Saul,
from my new home and workstation,
beautifully constructed in meleke,
yellow Jerusalem stone,
glowing gold in rising and setting sun,
a safe, environmentally friendly neighborhood,
Jerusalem rebuilt and temple standing,
could not help observing,
that military camps of world police,
around the holy city were accumulating.
If the times of peace were truly upon us,
why here of all places?

And in the tales of friends from around the world,
I learned that this buildup was not uncommon,
though most had no apprehension, no perception
of what could happen if it all went bad.
Compliant media and every local politician,

in church and state agreeing,
extolled the virtues of our hero king,
many openly referred to him as such, a savior,
excoriated those who saw the mortal danger,
beating any who tried to give fair warning.
Yet state control was not the only sign
of things going wrong or gone:
the Babylon prophet, to discerning eyes,
looked more and more like the Nazi mouthpiece,
a Goebbels praising his and our Great Leader to the skies,
his own ambition clearly without limit,
the Great Leader's gifts flawless and consummate,
to be accepted and obeyed without question,
all questioning considered insurrection.

Who could or would doubt the validity,
of their designated social credit score,
the Leader's bureaucrats chosen very carefully,
by his proclamation indisputable and more.

Such was the ugly memory
of savagery of war just past,
most trusted blindly
that this false peace would last.
The wave of unseeing love and devotion,
fueled by false prophetic blind emotion,
meant criticism of any sort was dangerous,
unless his enemies were criticized,
what benefitted him must be good for us.

And though life outside my bubble
was for many grim and terrible,
I kept my mouth shut, what could I do,
whatever came next, I could not stop,
and if I lost all I had built up to now,
stranded in this place where he ruled,

my doom was certain.
The possibility of sabotage remained,
and anyway, perhaps I had been fooled,
perhaps the world would stumble on,
and good come of it all if we just trusted.

The resistance starts to form

Yet not all were as faint of heart as I,
nor had self-interest as strong,
Jewish believers especially,
but also, many others, before long,
declaimed the trend openly,
the more cautious treading softly,
indirectly, subtly raising issues.
But modern-day sicarii there were as well,
who even combined with Muslim fedayeen,
suspicious of the depth of Islam's fall,
now called him Iblis and great Satan.

The Great Leader seemed to regard,
the holy temple as his throne,
or at least his own possession,
with the priesthood managed partially
by the False Prophet's bureaucracy.
Would not the curse of Jeroboam and Uzziah
break forth upon the presumptuous,
or else was he truly the Messiah?
But why did those who seemed to think,
and say too much,
find their social credit score in red ink.
And what of renditions coincidentally,
of some, though not all, loud voices raised,
here one day, but next, gone mysteriously.

My own timidity I soon confirmed as wise,
the pattern evident and obvious to me,
and many others took the hint to flee,
before the full closing of the vise.
I had the full protection of my trade and mentor,
there was no need for me to worry yet,
smokescreens and half-truths my armor,
against detection of my growing doubt.

The halfway point for the peace accord approached,
and I knew very few believers,
Jew or Gentile, remained in the city or the land,
fled overseas to other places,
prepared for refuge by the prophetic band,
those who knew Scripture and the signs,
of approaching doom and tribulation.

But the masses who outnumbered them
were not aware, false media complicit
to portray control as true freedom,
designating credible rumors of dissent,
as irrational, mindless nihilism,
to be nipped in bud and bloom
so the Great One's plans could flower.

The False Prophet's reforms had been accepted,
a social credit system had been embedded,
by all but a sizeable minority,
those who saw tyranny unfolding,
whether in a frame of eschatology,
or merely secular understanding.

And to my shame, I Saul, helped build
the technology that soon enabled,
quick recognition of those to be disabled,
withdrawal of their right to sell and purchase,

their human rights severely compromised.
I tried to limit the excesses I could detect,
and created redundancies, like holes in a net;
but even my leadership was compromised,
compartmentalized so sabotage was difficult,
the danger of detection manifest,
the penalties for deviation unclear,
but little doubt they would be fatally severe.

But none could see the entire picture,
save the Beast and his closest acolytes.
Perhaps I, Saul, saw more than most,
enough to make me realize the dangers,
began to prepare avenues for flight.

A dictator must rule the economy,
but many had developed work-arounds,
grey and black economies,
markets where the social credit failures
could survive off each other in perpetuity.

But dictators remain in power
by staying a step ahead:
he prepared the ground, proactive,
designating any alternative
as economic terrorism,
declarations of financial civil war
by selfish fools wanting to seize power.

The only solution which would stop
such disloyal prevaricating,
would be to dedicate each person's body,
confirm their true allegiance to the cause of peace,
by a mark on the hand or even face,
to show their full acceptance,
make them subject to his generous grace.

And even better, it was mooted,
the mark could contain a new ID,
guaranteeing only the worthy prospered.

Many, perhaps most,
clamored for this opportunity,
to show their true, unfeigned fidelity.
But alongside this fervor of faith,
a harsh yet unspoken accusation,
the unfaithful doubters of his reforms,
were Christians and Jews whose declaration
of Christ and his kingdom were at odds
with the plans and purposes
of these little gods.

So, every attempt by the Christ-lovers,
to circumvent what they knew would come,
was used by their enemies,
to undermine, subvert and disarm;
their credibility lost,
smothered
the message of true freedom.

Yet had grown a force to counteract
the corrupt propaganda:
the 144,000 had great impact,
brought salvation and empowerment to many,
though soon to be hunted mercilessly,
they and those who were converted.

The counterstrike subtly impugned their motivation,
because of them the sanctity of the temple was at risk,
of becoming less than sacrosanct, endangered,
of being overtaken by an antisocial sect.

Such shallow charges gave power to the one,
who coveted the temple for his throne,
through legislation piece by piece,
he prepared a legal, spiritual channel,
for full, unbridled access to the holy place.

The Jewish priests were not unaware,
of these machinations,
they prepared a strong resistance,
readied families and friends,
hoping for the best, suspecting worse.

And so, the world hung in suspense,
earth-dwellers and faithful alike;
would the reprobate cooperate,
those who sought to best God's elect,
would they, could they see the light,
if not, what was their judgment fate?

The believers in that age were not confused,
they read the signs of the times right and true,
battle on they must for the Beast arises,
could any flesh be saved from his dread master?
Yet those dark days, though dire, God shortens,
the future is unsealed and war will follow after,
against the elect, impressed with holy seal.
Leopard, Bear, Lion, jaws and claws of steel,
bowing to the Dragon who will make his head to heal.
False peace offered so he would be worshipped,
but time is up and his true face revealed.

8 DESOLATING ABOMINATION

c. 2033 AD

Saul meets one of the 144,000, named Ichabod, who instructs him on what is coming and presents the gospel to him a third time.
Soon after, the storm breaks in Jerusalem especially, but also in all Israel and around the world. The Antichrist definitively accepts the False Prophet's call for his adulation and establishes himself as autocratic world ruler.

The great miracles associated with the rescue of the resisting Jews (most of them) from Jerusalem (and the rest of Israel) occur and sightings of the warrior angel of the Lord lead many to think the Messiah has come. Saul does not identify with the Jews fleeing to Bozrah, instead he leaves with Ichabod. They set out for New Chicago, which has become one of the North American hubs of the Babylon system.

The peace process of that most turbulent of times
had nearly reached the halfway stage;
three-and-a-half years had seemed an age,
and the world held its breath and hoped,
that, fragile though it be, the peace would last,
the backward-looking resistance would be past,
the Great Leader's glorious vision fulfilled.

I shared the fear, who could avoid the tension?
Yet I could not believe such hope ill-founded,
my tentative steps to regain my freedom
already arousing occasional suspicion.
Another fear had also raised its head,
a pervading antagonism to the temple,
or rather to those who seemed in charge of it,
the Jews, and some references, not deferential,
to my Jewish roots.

My mentor, a false prophet, a little antichrist,
still blind, seemingly,
to my budding insurrection,
reassured me that, come what may hereafter,
my heritage was not a problematic matter,
if I stayed true and worked loyally,
always for him and his great master.

After one such disturbing interview,
while walking absent-minded, doubt following doubt,
distracted in the rebuilt souk,
another critical encounter took me by the throat,
and shook me inside out.

By chance again, yet I knew it was not,
I met a fellow Jew, one of the many,
with a strange name, Ichabod,
yet a firstfruit unto God.
As I knew most believing Jews
had already left the land,
and especially Jerusalem,
I felt a hesitation in this very public place,
to be seen even acknowledging this one,
who had a very public face.
Well-known for his criticisms,
accused of fomenting harmful schisms,
among the Great Leader's loyal masses,
pursued relentlessly but always escaped.
He and all his kindred worldwide
seemed empowered and protected.
Beyond all reasonable expectation
always anticipated presciently
the tricks and traps of their enemies,
found a way even when betrayed,
to turn the tables on the delatores.

We, Jon and Sarah, briefly intervened,
"Dear Paul, do you not see,
that your relationship to Ichabod
was somewhat like ours to you?
Did you feel overwhelmed
by his greater wisdom and protection,
he and his kin seemed impervious to harm,
greater than you, beyond your comprehension?"

Paul only smiled and said
"I had no opportunity to so reflect;
danger was imminent and I glad
of any help that I could get,
to find my way through the moral maze,
that every single life decision
presented in those days.
I did not know then
if they were immortal yet,
or protected by divine fiat,
they were simply one more unaccountable fact,
one that had potential for my survival.
But be patient, children,
there are stranger things to tell
which answer better your heartfelt question."

Paul resumed his tale.

I stepped outside the money changer's shop,
where I had exchanged
some old dollars for new credit,
the old currency nearly dead,
and he was there, simply looked,
and after my initial hesitation,
without a word I knew to follow,
gave no hint of recognition.
By backstreet and alleyway he led me,

till we came to a dark lane,
with no CCTV.

"Saul", he said, seemed to know me well,
I him only by reputation,
and wanted poster,
"Their use for you is nearly done,
and it is not what you believe.
I wish you could be secure,
in the faith of Abraham our father,
in Yeshua as your Lord and Savior;
but know, God has plans nonetheless,
for you and many other proselytes.
Close as you are to full faith,
death now would mean your dissolution,
and death is now closer,
it and sin crouch at your door,
seeking to manipulate
all your indecision.
Choose life, choose soon,
if you would flee the coming wrath,
make Christ your Lord,
receive Holy Spirit,
and all will be revealed.
But meet me here just before midnight,
the last of us are leaving.
We planned this flight for many months,
will have many vehicles, even helicopters,
at and around Hadassah on Mt. Scopus,
many others set up in every open space,
the British cemetery, playing fields and courts,
we will escape the coming genocide he plans."

With that he left me, standing mouth agape.
What was he talking of? I knew the Leader's plans,
so I thought; surely I would have some intuition,

close as I was to some in the Leader's administration?
Yet my conscience pricked me,
what if I was wrong; worse,
what if his fanatic kind and he
had truly read the situation,
I could be in danger,
as well as all my chosen nation.

Better safe than sorry, was my final decision,
resolved to pack necessities just in case,
my feet followed his thought,
yet I found myself lost in translation,
my double-minded will trapped again.
I would have to trust his claims,
his offer of security,
but who could guarantee,
safety in this world I helped design.
Conflicted, indecisive, yet again,
I walked my weary, worried way back home.

In this cloud of fear and doubt,
I walked into my apartment,
and who was sitting waiting there?
My mentor and the Antichrist!
Struck almost dumb, frozen,
never had I spoken to the Great One,
though at times had been in his vicinity.
Not over-large in body,
yet lean and strongly built,
like an ancient fighting general,
with, it seemed, a blend
of compassion with fighting spirit,
though some thought a touch effeminate
(those fool enough to say so disappeared).
Velvet glove contained a mailed fist,
a being not only seen and heard, but felt.

Now my heart and head
were overwhelmed by that presence,
all my defenses shattered in a look;
his eyes pierced through the veil I thought my protection,
read me like a book.
So, I thought, in my consternation,
yet his word to me was full of consolation.

"Dear Saul, I have heard so much about you,
value highly your contribution,
to all we have achieved,
bringing light to the world
through our work in this nation."

My mentor spoke then,
his words like balm of healing,
encouraging and engaging.
"Saul, we elevated you to high position,
knowing full well there would be strenuous opposition
to our work and yours and, as of late,
forces of evil seeking to undermine
the brave new world we would create.
We know they have tried to draw you in,
(my heart skipped a beat or two)
but we observe you have resisted this great sin,
uncompromised till now are you,
still loyal to us and our great vision."

The Great Leader leaned forward, conciliatory,
his gentle smile lowered
any guard I still possessed,
"Tell us, faithful Saul,
can you help us neutralize their plan,
so our good purpose may come to fruition?"
There was no protection
for my mind, heart or spirit,

all at once I, full of unthinking trust
in their good intention,
blurted out with a sob
every detail I could recall,
of my meeting with Ichabod,
as in a dream I revealed all,
quite unaware of the betrayal.

Satisfied they stood and made to go,
their faces now set like stones,
spoke to the black-garbed guards
placed at my door and window.

Turned to me, their final word a revelation
of the depth of their iniquity and mine.

"Foolish were you, treacherous Saul,
to think you could deceive us at all;
from the very beginning you were played,
a broken toy which we may now discard.
Every protection and plan you thought you had,
set in place by us, to lead to this objective,
the capture of just one of our real enemies,
and you the bait and hook to his destruction.
There is no hope for you, never was,
realize you've worked your own damnation."

Left me in horror to decipher,
the meaning of treachery and more,
encoded in my two-faced indecision,
which led to Ichabod's and my destruction.

For certain now, near was my end,
whatever they had planned,
bode not well for us nor any Jew,
determined to destroy the faithful few.

My mind clear now, or so I thought,
I considered blaming God or his messengers
who could have fought,
more boldly and openly to protect
me from the onslaught
of this False Prophet and the Beast.
Yet soon discarded that shallow thought,
"Take your own responsibility,
or come whimpering to nought!"

Resolved I became, to overcome the lie,
now the spell was broken,
one way or another, to do or die,
no matter what, my life was just a token.

Yet what could be done?
Smart and agile were the guards,
not stupid thugs but dedicated fighters.
I must simply wait for a chance,
sensed an opportunity would come,
to make some small amends.

When morning came,
after the tortured night,
dragged to a truck full of bewildered Jews,
many from the temple compound,
and next to the only empty seat,
kindly-faced Ichabod.
I hastened to apologize, tried explaining,
with a gentle wave of his hand
he stopped all my chattering.

"Few could have withstood that great assault,
on your soul and spirit,
you are not so much at fault
as you think.

None like you who know not new birth,
nor the power of Holy Spirit,
could stand against that wave,
that ocean of evil, and resist.

"In fact, to you we must apologize,
to disinform we used trap of the trapper,
to disarm some of his fell purpose in these days,
you have been his and our unwitting lure.

"Always, Saul, in his fell design,
for your Jewish blood you were drawn in,
bait to lure at least one of the firstfruits,
to destroy what he perceived to be God's plan.
We knew what the outcome would be,
gave you true but misleading information,
with plausible deniability
that you might be our tool for his deception."

This was my opportunity, to recriminate,
instead, I took it as a chance for some redemption,
forgave freely, still considered my betrayal of the saint
for what it was, ugly treason.

As we drove, under heavy guard,
I noticed that even beyond my former observation,
the city now heavily fortified
the whole central area surrounded,
from Olivet to Ein Kerem,
from Mt. Scopus to Ramat Rachel,
a ring of men and steel
with checkpoints already erected.
Clearly this was to keep the people in,
not from an outside enemy protected,
but subject to the enemy within.

Ichabod continued,
"But the troops found no helicopters
around Scopus Hadassah,
no assembled refugees at all.
When they captured me
waiting for you, in the souk,
caught by surprise, or so they thought,
I carried information that revealed
where the *real* escape would be.
Deceivers they are but double deceived
they will be,
God's purpose will not be frustrated,
now or in eternity.
And we will soon escape this death trap,
as will many others fleeing,
our God's great trap is closing."

Scarcely had he spoken,
than events precipitately moved,
as our prison truck took the Jaffa Road,
just by Davidka Square,
a group of Jewish radicals,
nicknamed Zealots by the press,
attacked the truck in force,
to rescue their arrested friends,
and us, as well, by happy chance.
The world police in a van following,
opened fire without warning
but were cut down straightaway.
The zealots had set up an enfilade,
the guards on our truck soon overpowered,
though several prisoners killed preemptively.
We all whisked away
in nondescript stolen cars,
soon swapped just five kilometers
from the ambush scene,

in a covered parking space,
at Malha Mall, all done with time to spare,
with helicopters, world police and an armored car,
only just converging on Davidka square.
The Zealot group dispersed with all their kin,
but gave us some cash,
now almost useless and devalued,
and left us a small car to get away in,
left over because of those killed in the van.
"Shalom, behatzlacha," they said with a grin,
and then we were alone.

Before we left the mall we changed our clothes,
and our appearance as best we could:
a little coloring on the skin,
our hair cropped close, sunglasses,
unshaven,
with new electronic devices,
and provisions just in case
we had to move through the deserts.
Not much else to do in those brief moments,
but we would never pass ID inspection.

I wanted to get to Haifa port,
had friends who could help, perhaps,
to get lost at sea on a merchant vessel,
concealed for a time, perhaps,
but Ichabod had other plans in place,
and soon enlightened me about
the true significance of this hour.

"Saul, not for nothing was your seeming betrayal,
nor my entrapment by your apparent treachery;
the information they extracted about the withdrawal,
led them to think you were a tool of disinformation,
as you were.

So they reset their trap around a stage-managed decoy,
Hadassah Ein Kerem,
ten kilometers to the west of Scopus, Jerusalem.
All has been ammunition against this great enemy,
to leave now somewhat unguarded
the true original site for evacuation.
But timing will be critical,
we know Antichrist will soon move,
we await the prompting of God's Holy Spirit,
he will touch more than one prophet,
and then we will go to a place that
Scripture has declared,
has been prepared.
That place will be a haven,
for Jews who do not believe, many
who oppose Antichrist but eyes not open.
I will go and minister to them there,
until that great day when our Savior will appear,
in glory as the victorious King of kings.
Come with me and receive
the promise of his protection."

I was of two minds, again,
torn between the promised surety
and the danger which was entailed in
the long journey home, to uncertainty.

The old me said, take the smooth road,
but out of the depths of my shame
I decided to chance the dangerous game,
felt a little relieved of my load.

Before Ichabod answered,
we both became aware,
of much shouting and cries of terror,
distant explosions filled the air.

He checked his media device,
to see what report was made,
and found we were demonized,
as traitors and murderers portrayed.

The attack on the prison convoy,
had become a cowardly ambush
of young recruits for the world police,
who had been tortured and murdered
by a coalition of those who clung
to their old religion and its warlike ways.
Innocent bystanders had been killed,
babies too; the terrorists apparently shrugged and said,
collateral damage, we are justified.
They were being hunted down, but more,
this open evidence of sedition and revolution,
required an iron fist from a secure seat of power,
which could enforce a true humane religion.
This was to be Antichrist and False Prophet's hour,
never let a good crisis be wasted,
especially not the one you created.

And so it happened,
desolating abomination in the holy place,
covenant of false peace cast off midweek,
three-and-a-half years to the day,
sacrifice to God replaced by the idolatrous
worship and vainglory he always seeks.
His armies of fear surround the holy city,
all Israel who resist receive no pity;
into the place prepared they can but flee.
Yet there would be at last a consummation
poured out quickly on all his desolation.

Any aware observer could tell for sure,
that all these events had been well planned,

in advance:
the Temple precincts clear,
and the Antichrist and his prepared minions,
established his seat of government right there,
defiling the holy place by his priestless presence,
erecting a statue of himself on the altar,
the ensign of the Dragon very near.

Led by the False Prophet,
the acolytes worshipped him;
a corrupt world quickly took up the strain,
rushing headlong, finally, yet again,
into the bottomless abyss of idol worship,
led by panic, fear and pain
to the slavery of a biochip.

By this great usurpation,
of all power on the planet,
he planned to destroy all opposition,
effectively, true church to be exterminated.
If that woman could be destroyed,
and all who might come to new birth,
who could Christ come for
on a hell-dominated earth?

Everything else required soon fell,
or rather put in place,
prepared in advance by many like Saul,
the promised system of transaction,
a mark effective to make distinction,
between those who would not,
and those who would with no hesitation,
follow the Beast,
now an official and familiar designation.
They also gave worship to the Dragon,
his true god and archon.

Those who would not take the mark,
if believing Christian or Jew,
must suffer brief trial and execution;
those who claimed another faith or none,
yet consent withheld,
could not work or trade,
were forced to be indentured,
for better or worse to those
by the Beast and Dragon captivated.
The indentured were marked on the left hand,
the right hand and head reserved
to mark the true faithful of the Antichrist,
those with no mark subject
to instant, intense interrogation.
So many rounded up
in that great dragnet well prepared,
that not all who were condemned to death
could be immediately executed.
Large workcamps, ready built,
became the hubs of slavery,
a not-so-sudden slide
from the old ways of democracy.

A new machine also unveiled,
portable, for tidy execution,
of those faithful who refused
to take the mark,
and offer an oblation, decapitation,
Madame Defarge could not keep pace.
And the pace was worldwide,
in every center of New Babylon's power,
the pattern was repeated:
in many places an image and an altar,
worship and offer homage,
take the mark, obey your Lord,
worship his guiding spirit, the Dragon,

come into this wholly renovated world,
or suffer short and sharp extinction.
And though many had been taken
into custody preemptively,
soon indentured or enslaved,
many chose the grim alternative,
submitting openly, willingly to the death machine,
a faithful witness of their faithful king,
fearless in martyrdom.
But most went into hiding,
one way or another,
some survivalist, some dependent on
an uncertain neighbor,
some into indenture.

But as Ichabod later described to me,
Not everything went the beastly trio's way,
their support in first heaven was cast down,
in humiliation;
Satan and his army, yet another step too far,
hubris through the Antichrist's temple desecration,
precipitating eviction by archangel Michael's spear
and the matchless legions of heaven.
Now demons restricted to the earth for a time,
confined spiritually but in forms diverse and physical,
turning life on earth into a living hell.

So, many saints survived, protected by both God
and many He inspired, among the unconvinced,
those hesitant to believe the truth of Christ,
yet reluctant followers of the newly-minted tyrant,
some even actively opposed.

And the Jewish people fled Jerusalem,
and all Israel as it happened,
though a few remained to serve the golem,

(as those Jews opposed now presciently called him).
Reprobate Jews pledged to the Beast as if he was Messiah,
justifying his unholy desecration.
Most Jewish people who could fled the city,
or at least tried to flee,
but many soon taken into captivity.
Most would be sold into a reinvented slavery,
but many faced public execution
on trumped-up charges of insurrection.
Still, many escaped the clutches of the world police,
into a long prepared safe place.

The evacuation from Hadassah Jerusalem a success,
with many vehicles great and small,
small cars, buses, trucks,
nondescript and government labelled,
even helicopters ferrying refugees,
a mass rescue like Dunkirk by land and air,
few police or military to hinder their escaping,
most lured elsewhere by Ichabod's disinformation.
However, they still faced a cordon around the city,
and missiles could destroy the hopes of many.
Those who fled on foot or any vehicle,
were faced by a ring of steel,
guns pointing inward.
Yet most had heard the news,
head for the garden and the Mount of Olives,
the word is that we will see a great deliverance.

And so it was: the ring of steel broken,
the Beast's police and army, all their communication,
shattered by an earthquake of power very focused,
shook the entire city, split the Mount of Olives.
Especially in that place,
the enemy's line was broken,
the grateful Jews poured through the gaps,

heading to a predetermined destination,
and on the way some said they saw a vision,
a mighty angel of the Lord, sword drawn,
could it be Messiah?

The place of their protection,
the subject of prediction,
thousands of years before.
All the hills north of Wadi Rum,
well known to Lawrence,
the Bilad al Sharat full of tunnels,
between Petra and Basira which is Bozrah,
a refuge in which was set great store.
Both Jewish and Muslim rebels
had conspired for many a year,
to build a city maze underground,
helped by the discovery opportune
of many ancient refuges long forgotten.
This complex could withstand any attacker,
though all knew they would still be dependent
on divine protection,
the same that brought them there.
For even on the way to their place of refuge,
the forces of the Beast tried
to exterminate them in a flood.
As those on foot hastened along highway 90,
to reach the choppers assembled
for them at Bar Yehuda airfield,
trapped between the wall and the salt sea,
the enemy poured every drop of water,
from dams and reservoirs,
newly-opened springs from the earthquake,
channeled down,
by reckless bombing created
a much deeper channel from Kinneret,
increased Jordan's flow manifold.

The flood waters rose rapidly,
the Dead Sea rising visibly toward its old level,
threatened the children of Israel,
but the threat soon receded,
with a minor aftershock rumble,
the rift opened further, deepened
and the less salty sea returned to its lower level.

Many wondered why their cruel enemy
did not simply bomb and strafe their helpless column,
he had tried but the bombers just exploded,
in midair and on the ground.
Later he would try again,
with huge daisy cutter bombs,
to destroy the cave system,
to suck the air and life
out of his opposition,
but the same result: they had divine protection,
the bombs just exploding, inexplicably,
in aerial detonation.
All these events might have been foreseen,
by Ichabod and his kindred,
but events had moved too fast even for him,
caught at the center of the maelstrom,
and so the Spirit touched his heart,
"Go with Saul and save him!"
I, Saul, of course, was grateful beyond thanks,
and willingly accepted his companionship,
any faith I had badly shaken,
but trusted the saint's belief on my behalf.

Ichabod said,
"We will make it to your home in Illinois,
but great peril awaits in the coming years.
For times, time and half a time deep tribulation
will intensify as the scroll is unsealed.

White, red, black, pale, the horses of destruction
will go forth still to wreak fair judgment on the world,
and the tribulation saints, who do not yield
will feel the full force of Antichrist unleashed,
his rage in a judgment of death revealed.
Their souls will join those under the altar of God
robes whitened in the Lamb's pure blood.
But the great red dragon will ultimately fail,
carried to refuge in the air the glorious lady,
protected Israel,
his purpose to destroy her children foiled,
as earth and heaven make conspiracy.
Earth has swallowed flood,
and manna will fall from heaven,
and though in rage he wars against the brethren,
Michael will yet protect God's Messianic children,
from Satan's threatened genocide.
O witness all these things, our Lord above,
and raise your martyred saints to the throne of love."

9 GREAT TRIBULATION

c. 2033—2037 AD

Saul and Ichabod make it, miraculously, to New Chicago, despite the extensive security system the Antichrist has in place, but that is another story . . .

New Chicago, after the considerable nuclear damage to New York, has become one of the North American hubs of the Babylon system, like the head of an octopus in the heart of the North American continent. Mexico City is the other North American hub, controlling the West Coast, Latin America down to Panama, and the Caribbean.

The Jewish leader introduces Saul to a mixed group of Messianic and Gentile Christians, and associated groups fighting the Antichrist—many old school atheists, jihadists, and zealots. He discovers the believers' elaborate network to circumvent the Babylon system. He finds out it was being set up even before the hidden rapture. There is also a network of support for Christians amongst unbelievers who have taken the mark or been forced to take it, many of whom are or were Muslims, but there is always the danger of betrayal since there are strong incentives for delatores. He is surrounded by death and destruction and martyrdom as the Antichrist and False Prophet have declared war on the true church, and the Antichurch and the world police and military are now hunting down professing believers of any sort. The penalty is always death by decapitation.

Saul observes the cleverness and guile of the teachings of the False Prophet and his acolytes, and their relationship with the Antichurch. He is surprised by some of the churches which are willing collaborators with the Antichrist, having been deceived (by new age teachings etc.) into believing that the Antichrist is indeed Christ, or at least that his program is in accord with the gospel.

The deceptions work in reverse on him and gradually lead him closer to a commitment to Christ.

False Christ and False Prophet, once seeming fair,
now acting foul, mouths open in blasphemy,
revealed their anti-God and anti-Church intentions,
to a roar of rapturous applause from their acolytes,
thoroughly steeped in his foul doctrines,
now filled with bloodlust against his enemy.

But the faithful show no fear, falsely accused
condemned to sword and captivity.
One popular prophecy proclaimed:

"You are forewarned, my people, show patience,
though an idol image speaks false pretense,
be not deceived by mammon's pseudoscience.
Doomed are the lawless sons of perdition
by His fiery breath and the brightness of His coming."

And I, Saul, and Ichabod, through many a danger
and testing of our mettle,
arrived at last by covert means in New Chicago,
changed in appearance and character,
especially I, Saul.
Though the veil still remained over Yeshua,
I now knew without a doubt
which God I would live and die for.
Ichabod treated me like a proselyte,
perhaps presumptuously,
yet every seed planted in my mind and heart,
would soon bear great fruit spiritually.

And in the world, poisonous seeds were sown,
from seven hubs with the immense New Babylon
controlling all,
in North America,
New Chicago ruled the East, North and center,
Mexico City the West and South to Panama,
and the Caribbean.

Though much had been destroyed in civil war,
old boundaries redrawn on continental scale,
priority was given to restructured communications,
though many still went hungry without shelter,
the world police could move fast in all directions.

I, and even Ichabod, were amazed,
at the size of the majority
who gladly served
the Beast's system and his authority.
Many would become enraged
at the least countersuggestion
that the Beast and his False Prophet
were anything but a divine intersection.
And then we had to run for cover,
there was only one consequence,
no trial, only the word of a delator,
would mean the loss of our heads.

Yet capture was not inevitable,
resistance, though dwindling by the day
through attrition and betrayal,
was still strong and not just among believers.
Many old-school atheists, jihadists
and sicarii, destroyed Babylon's infrastructure
where they could, jamming and deleting
information tech and storage, data centers,
from Hohhot, China, to the Citadel, Nevada,
creating gaps and holes in the data systems,
ripped nets through which many could escape.

And I discovered something never seen or known,
which my parents no doubt had a hand in,
a worldwide network of believers out of sight,
and many who had taken the mark
yet hated the Antichrist,

an underground developed over many years,
which fed and housed, when persecution came,
had safe houses and safe systems,
alternative economies to mimic or bypass
mark-based transactions.
And those filled with regret, and anger,
who had taken the mark and made obeisance,
realized the full consequence only later,
now rebels.
And many from places of indenture,
helped those with no place to go, the saints.

Inevitably some who were caught
would betray the rest,
for any delator the reward could be great,
possession of the property of the betrayed,
not to mention a greatly enhanced
social credit score.

So, for several years the war proceeded,
though from most of the Beast's acolytes
the true holocaust concealed,
living well his faithful supporters,
off the blood of bitter persecution.
Yet he was unable to defeat,
his entrenched enemy at Bozrah;
nor could he ever capture any
of the firstfruits of the Lord.
The miracles of protection made it plain
that too many losses would reveal
his lack of omnipotence to all,
so he focused his intent malign,
on ordinary believers, Jew and Gentile,
to destroy church and purpose divine.

Miracles of blood and fire he performed,
through the False Prophet, his chosen,
who persuaded many,
to believe the Beast was the promised One,
Messiah Christ, by God appointed,
dooming his opposition to destruction.
And though it was manifestly clear,
his true god was the Dragon,
most had no resistance to the great deception,
they flocked to his banner.
And the Beast became a familiar name,
a sobriquet to describe the unconquerable,
so they thought, for a time,
though anyone who added 666,
became carrion for wild dogs
that roamed the streets.

Yet many heard the word of the true prophets,
had nurtured seeds sown in their hearts
before the conflagration;
they came into the faith in millions,
death often the price for their salvation.

Most chose to avoid the extreme penalty,
as long as they could survive the deprivation,
but many rushed to witness, proclaiming boldly,
martyrs torn apart by mobs but some conversion,
eyes forced open
by the bravery and faith of the saints,
even in their painful destruction.

So the church was not as much reduced,
as the False Prophet's plan had intended.
Still, he had many of the old corrupt religious,
who proclaimed from church and synagogue,
mosque and temple,

the worthiness of this new savior of the world,
and the worthiness of fundamentalists for death,
whose faith was the damnable folly of the simple.
Many such corrupt were used to lure,
those new believers who had no discernment yet,
to their destruction, dragged into the Dragon's net.

How could such seemingly good religious,
our once-were brothers,
whose confession of faith had seemed the same,
now betray even friends,
to death and destruction,
even whole families?

It was no longer possible,
to have theological discussion;
but it became evident that many,
through biblical illiteracy,
and not knowing Holy Spirit
were easily blinded by deception.
The seeds had been planted long ago,
no matter how, they came now to fruition.
The old poisons had done their deadly work:
false separation of spirit and flesh—
Christ only *seemed* to die on the cross—
new gnosis paraded as Holy Spirit inspiration,
theosophical, raising spirits of the dead,
qabalistic, fatalistic, even stoic,
their minds like whirling dervishes,
spun into a vortex of perverse logic.
The Antichrist used such reckless folly,
building his Antichurch, with one main purpose,
to snare and betray the many,
yet his acolytes would also perish in his fire.

And I looking from outside, as it were,
was amazed at the wide range of once-were churches—
liberal, conservative, Episcopalians and Catholics,
even some Pentecostal and Reformed—
almost overnight seemed to give up the ghost
of the faith once fought for faithfully.
No doubt now they all believed,
most sincerely,
that to call the great leader *Antichrist* was sin,
for they said,
"So the Pharisees designated the true Christ,
called him false prophet,
even Satan's servant,
when he appeared in Galilee.
Our Beast must be the true Messiah,
he has only good fruit manifest!"
Even the Jews said so at first,
though most lately changed their minds.
They had, it's true, some excuse:
the mass media of the day
filtered all the news to hide the horror.
Yet blood was on their hands,
their own concupiscence,
lust for other things and power,
blinded them to the reality
of the mass murder they complicitly
supported and encouraged.

I, Saul, lost many faithful friends,
soon made,
soon disappeared,
every believer quickly realized,
there may not be many left to welcome Him
who would soon enough appear in the skies.
All knew, as Satan did,
three-and-a-half years were appointed,

from desolation of abomination
to the second coming in the cloud,
to sound the trumpets seven,
even grimmer judgment on the world.

Ichabod and others taught me much,
throughout those grim and fateful years.
I look back in derision at my own hesitation,
to see the truth of ages facing me,
fulfillment of prophecies all around,
the obvious reality of who Messiah was,
and is, and always will be.
And though the veil was not removed as yet,
I realized I was probably as Ichabod had been,
before the hidden rapture of the elect.

How did I survive such perilous times?
Probably by association:
Ichabod and the firstfruits, his brothers,
clearly had divine protection,
so to him and them I stayed very close.
Because of that close affiliation,
I seemed impervious to
the false prophetic deception,
the arguments and promises
of heaven on earth,
touched me not
but led me much deeper in,
closer, so close to the new birth.

And as the days and weeks,
grew closer to the time we estimated,
sign-seekers we were all, admitted,
but in those last days,
sign-seeking sanctioned by the word.

And then it happened!

10 THE SECOND COMING

c. 2037 AD

Great signs begin to appear, and Saul recognizes them as those his new friends have been telling him about. When the cross appears in the heavens he nearly yields and gives his life to Christ. But Saul's self-condemnation and hesitancy block his final acceptance of Christ and he misses being taken up in the open rapture, though the open rapture and the appearance of the Lord seated in the heavens leads to the breakdown of all his resistance, and with the mass of the Jewish people, in great mourning and repentance, he receives Christ as his Messiah, Lord and Savior.

But now he must endure the Trumpet judgments, and life becomes even more stringent and fraught as the Antichrist, knowing his and Satan's time is nearly done, cracks down even harder in an attempt to completely destroy the church. However, Saul hears the rumor of a new force arising, Two Witnesses, who have powers greater than the Antichrist.

We, Jon and Sarah cried out in astonishment,
"We held our tongues till now, but are amazed,
that world you lived in full of such hazard,
manifest evil in angels and humans resident,
we wonder you survived the grim assault,
but what could turn such bitter hearts back to God?"

Paul's countenance, full of peace and grace,
though underlying it sad memories,
glowed with the life of the forgiven,
said, "Hope, repentance, faith and salvation,
are something given, never earned.
No soul is ever lost
beyond hope of justification,
until reprobate, they die,

choosing and having chosen
death and eternal separation."

Paul then continued his graphic depiction,
of the tale of woe and judgment.
He said,
"This was now the time of the Sixth seal:
light of heavens would be withdrawn,
all nations distressed, what is to come?
"To earth had been cast down, twisted hosts,
both they and earth-dwellers
fiercely angry, yet afraid,
for more fearful yet the wrath of the Lamb.
Earth quakes yet they hide in a cave,
no cry of repentance, yet deliverance crave,
to sinful hopes they ingloriously cleave.
Islands will move and mountains will fall,
still, they refuse worship to the Lord of All.

"After a brief pause, calm before the storm,
the first trumpet sounded,
now no excuse for them.
Sign in the sky, look! The eagles gathered,
not in the desert nor in the inner room will He appear.
The voice of heaven will say, "Come out of her!"
Babylon will fall, O how it all falls dark;
glory to the Ancient of Days, do His work,
unless you worship the Beast with his mark.
Such must drink the wine of God's fearsome wrath,
in their drunken haze no saving path."

"Do you understand this," asked Paul,
"Those whom Scripture calls earth-dweller,
those who cling to the sin of the great Fall,
have no hope because they choose despair.
But know this and learn its lesson, Jon and Sarah,

even out of such darkness visible,
the Lord calls an elect, His will inscrutable,
yet always right and true, unbreakable."

He continued his narrative:
"Of all the signs at that time of open appearing,
two would bring me,
and almost every Jewish person,
those still living, to salvation,
though through an abyss of deep mourning.

"First a sign appeared in the high heavens,
bright celestial object, a clear cross forming;
the Antichrist's astronomers
said it was just a comet.
Yet many knew that could be disproved,
for it was seen from every place on earth
and never moved.

"The true prophets left on earth all declared then,
'The Son of Man in the clouds will soon appear,
quickly humble yourselves, O men,
to redemption you may still draw near.
But if you cling to your shaming of the Son,
you will be lost though the battle has been won,
doomed to your judgment of destruction.
He comes in like manner as He once went,
but His heavenly work is not yet complete,
so repent of your sins while you may,
there is still time to turn away.'

"Sad to say, I, Saul, was not quick enough to take the hint.
I, with all his people who had looked for signs,
throughout the history of our race,
was not impressed enough to fall directly on my face.

"And then we did . . .

"One day as I was in the market,
looked skyward to see the cross still in it,
though pale in the noonday sky so bright,
and soon every eye on earth looked with me.
A trumpet blast like none ever heard,
was heard by everyone alive,
and the dead in Christ.
Every eye looked up,
it came from above,
and as I looked a light transcendent,
slowly but persistently, incandescent
began to spread from the center of the cross,
became a glowing orb which made Helios
pale by comparison, though to the eyes
not hurtful, filled one tenth of the vault,
and in it one like a Son of Man,
seated on a throne,
and two resplendent beings stood by,
though in sackcloth garbed poorly.

"At first, He said no word,
yet we could not help but look,
his face a vision of love,
then held out his arms cross-like
and showed his palms, nail holes to prove
he is the one who rose from the grave,
Yeshua ha Mashiach.
He did not seem to speak but all heard,
the holy voice of heaven in their ears,
even the deaf perceived.

'These are my two witnesses,
listen to them, come to me, be saved!'

"The two witnesses then descended;
I cannot tell how, but as they did,
their form became more earthly,
less heavenly, yet beyond our flesh.
They would appear manifestly in Jerusalem,
direct challenge to the beast of Babylon.
"Yet even greater wonder:
as they came down to earth,
every living saint
went up in rapturous glory,
preceded by the martyred dead.
And when all had been gathered,
singing around his throne,
the vision of the Lord receded,
and the aura of the light of heaven,
yet the celestial cross remained,
a reminder of the vision
which could not be denied."

The Open Rapture

"So the Lord of All and true Christ
appeared in all His glory.
Seated on the throne came in the clouds,
summoned the faithful remnant,
all who remained from the killing fields,
all the firstfruits of his commissioning.
I saw Ichabod and many others rise up, glorified,
and every dead beheaded saint,
raptured openly to their Lord on high.
Neither I nor the tribes of Israel could longer deny
our true Messiah. Weeping grievously we sighed,
'See the holes in His feet and hands,
the great wound in His side,
our Jewish King of Glory abides
on the throne of heaven,

from which judgment and blessing will proceed.
Forgive us, Lord, now we know, your true identity,
now death is swallowed up for us,
in life and victory.'"
Many turn from the Beast to the Son of Glory,
receive the seal of God to turn His fury.

Saul Born Again

"I realized in a thunderclap of revelation,
how very selfish I had always been:
only child of a couple doting,
given everything, if not, reacting,
with sulks and tantrums negative.
In adulthood my choices narcissistic,
drawn to those like me, sociopathic.
Now I saw it all in grim perspective,
hell concentrated in a single soul
But, at last, the mighty hammer fell,
to break the carapace of She'ol.

"Finally, I Saul, was born again,
every last resistance shattered,
yet too late to be taken up, renewed,
my body still subject to the Trumpet woes,
and Dragon and Beast's last throw of the dice,
soon to unfold, even in their death throes.

"Yet now a greater peace,
than I had thought possible in this life,
permeated my spirit and my soul, my essence.
I sensed I was now free from the demonic,
those deep and dismal forces chthonic,
which ruled my old existence
in so many ways.
And latterly questions theological were resolved,

in a flash of brilliance unfolded,
revealed in the divinity of his face,
the true relationship of law and grace,
salvation for both Gentile and Jew.
As the Berber Bishop said,
'Our righteousness is only such as to consist
in the forgiveness of sins
rather than in
the perfection of virtues.'
Salvation and justification must be by grace and faith,
even our actions in repentance and sanctification;
yet the turn and saintly life result in good works,
good works subject to unaccountable rewards.
The conflict was resolved in his person,
he must be God,
for every act of faith requires God's grace.
The choice of faith to believe in Yeshua,
is not a good work at all,
though perfect fulfillment of the law,
because activated by the grace of God,
enabling us to walk unselfconsciously
in the law of Christ.
And deeper roots of faith are established
as a consequence,
to believe from the bottom of our hearts
God's fundamental goodness and omniscience,
that his grant of grace is not arbitrary,
neither casual nor whimsical nor contrary."

(Our faces brightened as Paul said these things,
each one's eyes filled with the light of revelation,
and each other's look deepened with profound concern
as Paul continued his narration)

"Yet not all hearts had been softened as mine had;
sad to say, harder still to believe then,

the fiercely orthodox at Bozrah,
clung to the old Talmudic line,
even the clear evidence in the air,
of saints openly taken up,
and the Lord on His throne,
did not meet their strict requirement for
a Messiah of a somewhat different tone,
one who comes riding set for war,
to destroy all the enemies of his people.
They said,
'Perhaps this is Him, but he has not come to earth yet,
we will wait and see.
We have been fooled enough for now,
by Dragon, Beast and False Prophet,
perhaps this is just another ploy,
to lure us to the destruction which they planned.'"

"Such hardheadedness and stiff necks," exclaimed Sarah,
"How could they be saved?
Yet I perceive," said after brief reflection,
"God's grace is unaccountably great,
sufficient for all our redemption and salvation."

And Paul continued,
"I myself was startled that the Lord,
did not immediately descend in great power,
but remained in heaven,
seated on the throne.
So too, the earth-dwellers, after a fearful pause,
believed the False Prophet's declaration,
that this was no divine enemy,
he, an alien invader,
did not invade immediately
afraid as yet to test their power.
The fear of the earth-dwellers became false hope,
that they and their Beast could defeat Him,

and led by the false prophetic claim,
set out to destroy entirely the enemy within,
those who still clung to the power of His name.

"And many there were who now believed:
the great mass of Jewish people had seen
the veil torn away for all,
though some manufactured a veil of their own.
All the elect of this time were sealed,
no earth-walking demon could afflict them,
yet still subject to gross physical humiliation,
and death by Babylon's decree,
mass decapitation.
But such threats had not been sufficient,
to stop a global revival event
not after the hidden rapture,
nor was it now, when all could see,
for those with eyes and ears,
who turned en masse,
the Jewish people most fiercely,
against the Beast and his unholy city.
Some of the Beast's inquisitors, even delatores,
turned away from their adherence
to the system of life and idol worship he adjures,
to the only One they could now trust
to bring salvation and deliverance.

"Holes in the net appeared often enough,
that many escaped the traps more than once,
and many there were who took the chance,
of helping those who seemed to have no hope.
And so, the church endured for a time and times,
though many perished in bold martyrdom,
and often enough earth's guilty denizens,
demon and earth-dweller,
were pitted against each other,

even brother against brother.
"And I, Saul, often slipped
through the chaotic cracks,
yet wondered how long
I could evade in this malevolent matrix,
the forces and power arrayed against me.
My hometown was a hub of the Babylon Six,
particularly, stringently, locked down by the enemy.

"Yet a whisper came to my mind one time,
in prayer and fasting many days,
as every saved soul had to be always,
a thought which seemed to defy all reason:
'Return to the place you fled in fear,
go back to Jerusalem,
the center of the Beast's global power.
I would have you there as a support
for those whom I have sent, ambassadors,
they challenge and make sport,
of the Beast and his commissars.
You, Saul will help prepare the way
for the warrior King who comes in glory.'

"I realized that in a lesser sense,
I took the place of Ichabod my mentor,
as he ministered in the Seal judgments,
so I would serve to the sound of trumpets.
I had heard the rumor of a new force rising,
stronger even than the combined firstfruits,
yet just two men called Witnesses,
equipped with ancient powers,
before whom the Beast and his court trembles.
I set out before the week was passed,
evidently into the jaws of death."

11 TWO WITNESSES

c. 2037—2040 AD

Many miraculous interventions occur and the miraculous provision and protection for the Jews at Bozrah continues. An immense worldwide conversion of the Jewish people, as well as millions of Gentiles, has occurred, and the believing churches become dominated by Jewish leaders as most of the Gentile leaders have been captured and executed. However, it becomes evident that the attrition rate of believers is high: some die in the natural disasters and, though none are destroyed by the demonic manifestations appearing in the earth, many earth-dwellers are. Saul has many adventures, getting to Jerusalem and then in the Temple, once he meets the Two Witnesses. While on the way to Jerusalem he has a dangerous encounter with a priestess of Babylon. He also hears in advance of the exploits of the Two Witnesses from a pilgrim out of Jerusalem, especially their encounter with the Antichrist and its consequences.

The Two Witnesses having taken the Temple and mortally wounded the Antichrist in the process, proclaim themselves Christ's ambassadors and declare the Trumpet judgments before they occur. They actively oppose the Antichrist forces and none dare interfere with their sovereignty in the Temple precincts. Although they are hemmed in closely, their message gets out in various miraculous ways, and Saul serves the Two Witnesses.

They declare Christ as Lord and Savior and prophesy his imminent return as King of kings and Lord of lords, rebuking and contradicting Satan, the Antichrist and the False Prophet. They also prophesy to their followers that God will soon allow the Antichrist to kill them all, but that God's church will be triumphant.

As the Trumpet judgments period draws to a close Saul is killed after seeing the Two Witnesses beaten as they are dragged out into the streets to be publicly executed.

There is a celebration of this apparent victory by the earth-dwellers but it will be cut short by the rapture of the Witnesses and the following events, especially the seventh Trumpet which they all hear.

Saul finds himself in heaven, as a martyr with a new name, being trained for his part in the imminent Armageddon invasion.

I journeyed, by many dangerous and devious ways,
back to Jerusalem,
into the heart of the world's darkness,
which also contained his promises,
I could not wait to meet them,
by some reports such greats as Moses
and Elijah.

And at this time, in heaven,
the seventh seal, unsealed in silence,
its import hidden,
but we knew the coming seven trumpets,
with much incense,
would answer the heartfelt prayers of every saint.
Noise, thunderings, lightnings, the earth quakes
again, even before the first trumpet speaks,
repent, the trumpets are the final chance!
Messiah's people all rallied at the sound,
heard even on the earth,
but would the Gentile nations turn around?

Although the vision of the Lord
enthroned on a cloud
had faded from our view,
though constantly in each person's mind,
for joy or terror,
the cosmic cross remained,
a constant sign fixed in position,
reminding all and affirming,
the testimony of the Witnesses.

11 Two Witnesses

Two ambassadors, plenipotentiary,
perhaps the thunders seven
spoke their names in heaven.
Two Witnesses in power and fiery testimony,
established their ministry in the inner court,
cleansed what had been polluted,
by Antichrist and False Prophet,
now instead of darkness visible,
light ineffable,
suffused the holy place, of all the holiest.

They shut up the heavens,
turned waters into blood,
fighting against all that hell-spawned brood.
The holy rally to them, to do or die in love,
and some like myself, always late,
attempted to break through the cordon of steel,
to join the companions of the Witnesses,
who carried out all their righteous commands,
servants of the servants of the Lord.

Yet all the saints who knew the Word knew well,
before the last and seventh trumpet has sounded
all saints and both Witnesses are destroyed.

The knowledge that our death in martyrdom was assured
did not deter the saints from being inspired
by the spirit of God and the Witnesses' declaration:
the Holy Gospel of salvation
to bring in many souls from every nation.
Many again rushed to martyrdom,
and the delatores and executioners welcomed them.
But most chose to walk in patient wisdom,
knowing their end but choosing,
to remain steadfast in the great harvesting.

I journeyed through the world to join them,
as Holy Spirit led;
but there were other spirits just as interested,
who sought my detention and destruction.
None were so enabled,
the seal of God my full protection;
but I learned much, understood at last,
why so many souls were reprobate.

One story sufficient
to show the depth of deception,
tangled web by False Prophet woven
on behalf of the man of sin.

Before I reached Syria,
through Izmir, Akhisar and Alasehir,
had cause to stop in Akhisar,
old Thyatira still in place,[1]
paused at the roundabout in the center,
amazed to see a new church,
or at least a church-like building
in that once Islamic town.

In retrospect I saw the deception
my tired, hunted mind could not apprehend,
the decorative recesses in the external stone
were very cross-like, seeming Christian,
yet the doorway arch shaped like a half-moon,
and in the floor beneath a star set, a hexagon,
a peace swastika in its center, a syncretism,
the pillars of the arch suggesting yoni-lingam.

Against sound judgment
I ventured through the door,

1. Smyrna/Izmir, Thyatira/Akhisar and Philadelphia/Alasehir, Antioch near Antakya.

sat in the seats, luxurious as they were
after all my privation,
in cool comfort took it in.

No one seemed present in the structure,
so I stayed a little longer,
trying to identify the nature of its religion.
Not only seats, with cushions to kneel on,
but an area of prayer mats,
facing into a large unlit recess,
which could be a sanctuary;
but no cross, only a banner
that could be an ensign,
rather like the flag of Wales.
It made my hair stand on end
as I realized its significance.
And before it stood, in the shadows,
hard to see with harsh window light behind it,
an idol of the Beast, that antichrist.
I tensed to stand and get out, too late,
a woman stood before me quizzically,
offered kindly to assist me if she could,
dressed in a vicar's black robe. Elegantly
it clung rather closely to her form,
arms bare, somewhat sensuous,
a collar around her neck, grey not white,
or was it Sillitoe tartan,
the custodian of this chapel from Hell.

I did not want to leave too abruptly,
fearing she might recognize me
from news of my past infamy.
I inquired the origin and purpose
of this place of worship, though now obvious,
and how she came to this,
such a small, undistinguished town.

The priestess, for so she was,
seemed very open to discuss
her history and how
she had come to minister there.
Sensing a possible opportunity
to share the gospel with one who had
no doubt been left behind,
I allowed her to continue,
looking for an opening to share.

"My friends call me Lily," she said,
"but my professional name is Lilith.
I was and am an ordained minister,
in the Christian church first,
and now better,
in this modern fulfillment of it.
I was one of those who did not believe;
though I had a degree in biblical theology,
my faith was shallow, fit for leaving,
the word of God a canard to my educated eye,
until the disappearing
(or rapture, as the unfaithful call it,
excuse my use of the word)
which opened up my eyes to reality.
I saw my own mother taken up.
Thunderstruck, I realized
how much I had to learn
of the great redemption plan.
The Christ was a real person,
not just a cosmic symbol,
who hung upon that cross."

(At this my mind was hopeful for her,
yet my heart advised great caution)

"His spirit rose from death
when the spear pierced his side,
how could I not have seen it,
that spirit now fully glorified,
has come back to us in earthly form,
our Great Leader wise,
more, he brings us redemption."

Breaking from my hopeful daze,
that she might be brought to salvation,
I hastened to interject,
"Surely you do not think this one
could possibly be the Christ?
If you have studied the word of God
you must realize he is the Beast."

A patronizing look askance,
full of pity, hate and despair,
at what she perceived as my ignorance,
put me on my guard, now fully aware.

"Foolish man, I have been inducted
into the lovely worship rituals of my Beast,
and now officiate myself,
well-equipped to school the foolish few
who reject truth so freely offered.
I have seen miracles of fire spectacular,
received the gift of prophecy—
indeed, this is called
the First Church of Prophecy—
my faith now founded
in a greater wisdom.
That wisdom is the key,
if you will only receive it,
you may have me and all my acolytes,
not to mention great enlightenment.

Realize that Christ and Antichrist are one,
that same selfless spirit who ascended
to the tenth level from the cross of plain wood,
that same emanation has come again
in power, to finally deliver us
from bondage to the law.
All the old opposites in the scriptures,
are fully reconciled in him,
open your eyes and ears
and let his spirit in."

As she said this last,
her demeanor became quite threatening,
but the spirit within her lost control
when I said forcefully,
"The Lord rebuke you,
spirit of Antichrist and false teaching,
spirit of adultery and immorality.
My true Lord, true savior, Jesus Christ,
born of the virgin's womb,
rose from the dead,
body, soul and spirit resurrected
from a cold stone tomb.
No pretender He but Lord of All,
the Lord rebuke you, Satan,
open not your mouth again!"

Her body tensed as if to spring in rage,
but instead collapsed, convulsing,
foaming at the mouth, spitting,
tearing her own flesh
with nails become like claws,
choking out vile blasphemies.

The Spirit whispered urgently,
"Run! Don't look back!"

I left hastily, victorious,
but with sadness in my heart,
resumed my journey.

And while eluding my executioners and bounty hunters
the word went out how the fugitive from Jerusalem
had dared profane the Beast's priestess and prophetess,
and tried to destroy his temple in Akhisar.

But I was able to evade them all,
for even in this old Islamic heartland
much had changed
since the second coming of the Lord.
Many new believers hid,
in the anonymity of each city,
living cooperatively,
often supported by other haters of Babylon,
who, though they lived in constant danger,
not only dared but actually sought out
fugitives like myself, their brother,
to succor and support.
Each cell of the faithful free,
each town-dweller and villager
operated independently,
passing me from one to another,
none knew exactly the whole chain,
of where I came or went.
Yet some died under torture, all remembered,
faithful to the end,
to their Lord and every friend of God.

Pausing to reflect and mourn lost saints,
at old Antioch near Antakya,
I met a man like myself, no marks on him,
a constant fugitive though, like me, protected,
a pilgrim from Jerusalem.

"We do not have much time," he said,
"but I am sent to spread the story
of how the Two Witnesses, holy men indeed,
destroyed the Beast in Jerusalem,
and what it means."
"The Beast is dead?" I exclaimed,
"perhaps we will be free?"

He shook his head,
and cited Revelation 13:3:
"Remember in his head
he receives a mortal wound,
but his deadly wound is healed."

Then his story he began to tell,
"My name is Michael,
a companion of the Witnesses
almost from the day of their appearing,
though where and how they first appeared
I do not know, I must confess.
Still, there is no doubt,
they are from heaven above,
sent by the King on His throne,
to proclaim and bear witness of
His great power for judgment and salvation.
I, Michael, met them on the road that led
toward the Temple built anew;
they called, empowered me to follow,
past every guard station on the road.
No miracle of concealment
which we all have seen before, I recall
they saw us clear enough, our purpose evident,
some even seemed to expect our arrival,
leveled their weapons instantly,
I thought that we would be
cut down in a leaden hail.

Believe when I say my heart nearly failed,
I saw and felt it, a roaring, searing fire,
twin tongues of flame
from their mouths consumed,
every guard post and their arms.
The troops who saw this happen
threw down every weapon,
they were spared,
but before we came into the Temple
many more were dead.

"All had fled from the outer court, so we went in,
to find none other but the Antichrist, the man of sin.
He and his entourage attempted a defense,
tried to call down fire himself but instead struck down
by the hottest flame yet from the Witnesses, so intense,
his arm was withered and his head burned deep in,
part-blinded, fell dead as a stone.
His image and the dragon idol were consumed,
I wondered that the False Prophet and the others had survived,
but the Witnesses commanded them to leave,
to take the body of the Antichrist away;
they hurried to comply.
I followed to see his ultimate fate,
hastened out by the West gate,
and then, in front of a great crowd,
all mourning and wailing,
the False Prophet underwent a change:
suddenly enraged and full of an ungodly power,
he laid the Antichrist on a bower,
cut himself and bleeding freely from many wounds,
chanted maledictions, curses and invocations,
and it seemed to all who watched and waited,
the Antichrist simply rose as if from sleep.
He did not say much but simply gestured
the False Prophet, now his voice, to persuade

the gathered multitude to worship,
which they promptly did,
with a devotion evidently crazed.

"But Saul, I saw more in the Spirit:
when the Beast's prophet had prayed,
I sensed a dark presence rising
as if from an abyss,
a spirit of death it seemed,
yet it reanimated the corpse.
I do not know what happened
to the life of the old Antichrist;
did it return to the body,
or is that body just a zombie cursed?
Now the pejorative golem really stuck,
but unlike those of the Baal Shems,
Eliyahu, and Loew ben Bezalel,
this monster will grow in evil beyond belief,
death written on its head,
no automaton, but Abaddon,
a vast, dark intelligence,
stewed from time's depth
in its own malevolence,
not for protection but destruction
of the Jewish race."

Michael concluded,
"So now, Saul, know this,
the power of our God in the inner court
cannot be denied.
The Witnesses are more than us, heavenly,
what we may one day be;
they are ambassadors of the Most High, plenipotentiary.
Serve them as well as you would serve God,
for His power rests within them,
to call down judgments on the earth
and all who dwell therein."

11 Two Witnesses

Armed with Michael's promises
I came at last to the holy city,
still sacred in my mind,
soon to be fresh and new,
though polluted overmuch by the Beastly crew.
Having walked most of the way,
across ocean and continent,
mountain and desert,
through Europe, Syria and Jordan,
I was somewhat thinner,
much changed by privation,
yet light in spirit as I approached
what I knew would be my final destination.

At last, I looked briefly down,
from a concealed location,
upon the Valley of Jehoshaphat,
where the final Armageddon battle
would be fought and judgment wrought,
on every unrepentant nation.

I knew the Witnesses had the Temple
under their control,
but surrounding all
a steel shield-wall.
Yet some went in and out freely,
despite the impenetrable armour of the Beast;
the rumor was, a guide would always come,
to lead the destined traveler through the gates.

I knew the way I preferred to go,
up on Zion's hill,
through the southern gateway, so
I made a loop around, crawling slowly down,
carefully through the many raised tombs,
aiming at last to go through Silwan

and the City of David,
hoping to find some unguarded tunnel access,
to bypass the South Gate
heavily fortified.
But before I arrived at the road
to Ma'ale Adumim, 417,
my guide found me among the dead.

All Jerusalem was locked up tight,
each road with its checkpoint;
just where I wanted to cross to Silwan,
guards and a ute
with a heavy automatic weapon.

As I awaited nightfall,
to optimize my chances,
the gentle golden glow
of sunset on those sentient stones,
a child wandering through the tombs
seemed to recognize me and said, "Saul,"
softly, with familiarity,
took me by the hand.
"Come with me,
follow closely,
remember Peter escaping Herod's captivity."

So, we walked in full view,
across the open road,
the guards looked but did not observe
the desperate criminal and his guide,
the long-wanted man, hunted,
who trespassed without mark or scan,
in the most secure place in the world.

Directly the child led me,
back along the open road,

through the Garden of Gethsemane,
up the hill and through the old Gate of Gold,
the east gate of the temple.
None of the many watchers paid us any heed,
we were invisible to their eyes,
the enemy convinced
there was some way underground,
his forces wasted searching, guarding there for spies,
while the saints walked free, unseen and protected.

As we entered through the outer court,
I wondering at the light
which permeated
every rock and stone it seemed,
when my guide just disappeared.
Some guards saw me then but drew back out,
when one of the Witnesses approached.
"Welcome, Saul," he said affectionately,
"we have been expecting you.
You will be one of the last witnesses
to record the grounds for
the final accusation of the great transgressor.
We are the ambassadors of God,
in the spirit of Elijah and Moses come
in these regenerate bodies to proclaim,
the power of God's kingdom,
the wonder of salvation and redemption,
declared throughout history,
before the cross and after,
to all who would listen and repent;
the gift of God through His dear Son sent,
all of grace and eternal life in joy and laughter,
all this dark rebellion
consigned to the Lake of Fire.
We declare the Trumpet judgments as they occur,
the Beast, though enraged, may not interfere,

the Dragon knows how near the end might be,
the return of the King imminent,
but seeks to forestall it murderously.
He longs to exterminate all witnesses,
us and the whole church, spiritually,
to forestall Christ's return as King of kings;
if the earth is laid waste of his followers,
how could His kingdom be?
But our enemy knows nothing of true kingship,
he should have learned servant cost
at the cross,
he also understands not at all true worship,
fueled by true love, not fearful obeisance.

"And so, we rebuke them, torment them,
provoke them to great follies,
declare the Trumpet judgments before they happen,
not least the three woes brought on themselves.
And we will use you Saul, from time to time,
to make our proclamations,
they cannot harm you yet, nor us,
until the time is up and God permits.

"When every saint has been destroyed,
the church seems devastated, eliminated,
and last of all witnesses we two,
whom he is given license to kill,
(God's will and plan not his)
the red line of transgression will be overstepped,
the guilty by their own mouth convicted,
doomed to the Lake of Fire, beyond She'ol.
He cannot, will not, understand
his choices lead inevitably, counterintuitively,
to fulfil what God has planned.

"Just as Christ rose from death,
so will His church
rise in glory and power,
clothed in pure white linen, armour enough,
to defeat His enemies in the last and greatest war."

And so it proved in the following months:
hail, fire and blood, a third of trees and grass,
great fiery mountain, a third of the bloody sea,
wormwood poisons a third of all fresh waters,
sun, moon, stars a third darkened in the day.
Woe, woe, woe to earth's inhabitants,
as angel key unlocks the deep abyss,
the seal of God from scorpions protects the saints,
yet a vast eastern horde kills a third of man,
still sorcery, murder, theft and fornication.

We, Jon and Sarah must have seemed very reflective,
filled with questions small and great
so, Paul paused to discuss and meditate
on what he thought our likely concern,
the depth of rebellion in every sinner,
not least every unrepentant earth-dweller
in those days, and their fate.
But I, Jon interrupted to exclaim
in some embarrassment,
"Paul, I know this seems a foolish question,
given the high and holy things of our discussion,
but I cannot help wonder at your provision,
confined as you were in the Temple,
with the Two Witnesses and however many others?
Did not the enemy have the inner court surrounded,
no doubt to starve you out,
and limit all your witness?
I have no doubt your answer will reveal,
not just prosaic means
but more miraculous provision."

Paul replied,
"Jon, your question is not foolish at all,
the grace of God and his provision
is revealed in the smallest detail,
of all our lives and needs,
nothing too prosaic for His attention.
For example, our enemy cut off
the waste disposal lines
which ran from several places,
yet the waste still disappeared as always.
I heard a rumor that it reappeared in other places,
let us say, inconvenient to our enemies.
And what about our food,
since the enemy shot anyone
who approached the Temple outer court,
let alone the inner court where we ministered?
In fact, we needed little food,
nor sleep if it came to that,
our worship and our work sustained us,
though, if any felt hunger
he could go at any hour
to a table near the eastern gate
of the inner court,
a board always set with delightful food,
in full view of every outside guard.
All ate better from that table's fare,
even in the shadow of death,
than they had for many a tribulation year.
None ever saw the food come or go,
but some said, 'Ask the crows, they will know.'
As for water, a spring bubbled up
from beneath the altar,
so refreshing, holy and pure,
tasted of the essence of life,
gave strength and courage too.

"But as I said, we did not need much food or sleep,
our service was a joy and blessing most sustaining,
the worship and the ministry sufficient to keep
our bodies and our souls full of life and laughing.
There were two dozen of us there at any time,
some came, some went, according to their purpose,
but always a cloud of glory over us.
And this pure worship was infectious,
those on guard for the Beast in the outer court,
would often come to tears and grief of every sort,
their hearts broken by the contradiction,
between their task and their heart's report.

"Many a message went to the outside, watching world,
through such deep ministrations to the lost,
the Antichrist slew many a converted guard,
such that the duty became a much-feared post.

"Yet this was not the only way the testimony,
of the prophetic witnesses went out.
They would regularly proclaim, in voices supernatural,
judgments, yet always with a repentance call,
and somehow their message always heard,
by a world terrified but fearful to believe.
Yet many did believe,
though faced with instant death,
the revival toll of martyrs mounting to the height,
getting closer to fulfillment, when the number
of the white-robed was complete.

"And I, Saul, was permitted to stay,
just as they had prophesied,
and soon enough we knew the time was near,
time, times and half a time completed,

"Just as there came a time two millennia past,
when God withdrew protection from His Son,
now his church, the ragged, glorious remnant,
Two Witnesses last of all to execution,
sacrificed on the altar of Satan's folly,
attempting to forestall the King of king's return.

And just before the end, or rather, the beginning,
I, Saul, had one last vision,
with John the prophet sharing,
of a rainbow angel who stands on land and sea,
face like the sun, feet pillars of fire,
he cries out, seven thunders reply,
yet sealed from us in measure.
He ate a little scroll from the angel's hand,
bitter sweet to take the prophetic stand,
time, times and half a time completed.
When the holy people are completely broken,
our enemies will believe that they have won."

The sixth trumpet heard,
the Antichrist demon armies are prepared,
not only will the church be destroyed,
but one third of all humankind
even those who sought the saints' destruction.

At this time the Two Witnesses declare,
their mission is complete,
they demand safe passage from the Temple,
as is for ambassadors appropriate.

But the malice of the Beast was only held at bay
by the power of God manifest in the Witnesses,
God's fiery power brought upon their enemies,
yet when unrestrained, evil seems somehow to hold sway,
the guards now under orders to take any opportunity,

to destroy those of the inner court, summarily.
After the first shots have effect without retribution,
My companion fell dead and I wounded,
they stormed the inner court, murderous culmination,
cameras record the consequence
of their stored fear and hate,
the world saw the Two Witnesses,
stripped, dragged naked, bloody, out.

Where I lay, my life ebbing away,
I saw the Two Witnesses
beaten, shot and stabbed many times,
barely recognizable, to the street dragged finally,
there to die painfully for all the world to see.
But the killers saw me watching and one,
with cruel visage, a twisted grin,
placed his revolver
against my head and pulled the trigger.

Yet they did not linger,
the Antichrist's executioners,
around the inner court,
sealed off the entire temple precinct,
hauled all the bodies quickly out
and threw them unceremoniously in a heap,
on the verge of Ha Ophel,
eager to escape
the condemnation of the light
which persisted in the temple.
So, the Beast did not try to reclaim
the temple as his own;
the light which shone in and from
the Holy of holies did remain,
an effulgent reminder and guardian,
for the One who would soon come to reign.

But, O how they celebrate, the Beast and his slavery,
dishonor the dead, those holy, just and true.
In Sodom and Egypt, brief pyrrhic victory,
true church seems gone, but always lives anew,
especially in that city where He bled and died,
earthquake, thousands die, one tenth destroyed
they give grudging glory to heaven's High God.
In fear they will hear the seventh trumpet sounding
and all will know, final judgment is soon coming!

And I, Saul, privileged with the few,
to be faithful to a martyr's death at last,
barely felt the pain, instantly made anew,
reborn, regenerated, mind, body and spirit,
welcomed by a thronging multitude,
not least my parents,
Johan and Miriam in glory,
though with new names.
My mind retained its earthly limits briefly,
but in moments I adapted to my new reality,
saw them and myself in our true, intended aspect,
the beauty and the terror
of my regenerate parents right there,
and me and every saint I had known well,
as beautiful and terrible
as any mighty angel.
Perfect harmony, standing before my Lord,
(along with all who perished with me)
Him whom I had always known distantly,
but who had always known me intimately,
in gentle aspect appeared.
Yet a sword strapped at His side,
a rod of white steel in his hand,
said those words I had longed to hear,
but feared that I might never,
"Well done, good and faithful servant Saul,

my gift to you a new name
engraved in white stone;
now you will carry me to many,
Christ-bearer, Paul."

I bowed my head in honor of His glory,
He raised it up again, with eyes like lightning,
said, "There is a battle yet for the fighting,
will you be part of my holy army?"

His request was my command.
I found myself involved
in intensive heavenly training,
for a battle both spiritual and physical,
to finally defeat His great enemy.
Armageddon (and the Millennium to come),
mere training grounds for eternal service
in the King of kings' great realm.

And though this training seemed to take many years,
from our place of bliss and light
we could still look down on the earthly vale of tears,
as in slow motion in mere days
came the judgment
on a world of hard-hearted reprobates,
for there in heaven, time and space
are different, more flexible,
we may bend them to our purpose,
yet still remain in the flow of life eternal.

12 BABYLON'S JUDGMENT

Sometime in 2040–41 AD, probably only a matter of weeks or days

The earth-dwellers see the Two Witnesses ascend, revivified, in a rapture-type experience, three-and-a-half days after murdering them, and soon after they also see an open vision somehow visible to all who remain on earth, a vision of an angel reaping. They recognize it means judgment on themselves, but harden their hearts in resistance, especially as the Bowl judgments proceed, cursing God all the while. Saul, now Paul, sees these events from heaven and marvels that no more repent; his friend Ichabod, now Davek Cabhod, of the 144,000, appears and explains what is happening and what comes next.

Paul and his friend continue to watch and see the fall of Babylon at the hands of the ten kings. Ichabod/Davek explains it all.

The Two Witnesses, Elijah and Moses,
stand before the eternal throne of God,
olive trees and lampstands,
bodies immortal can be harmed but never destroyed.
For three-and-a-half days
the earth-dwellers are fooled,
rejoice over the pyrrhic victory they achieved,
then amazed when their nemesis is revived.

Those unseemly dead bodies, broken,
which yet had not decayed
though naked, torn and beaten
suddenly in a great paroxysm breathed,
stood upright on their feet, healed and awoken,
in this new breath of life cried out
for joy in their immortal resurrection,
and the overwhelming love of their holy Lord.

No zombie resurrection this, as was the Antichrist,
but risen full of all God's power, all life and light,
to stand once more before the starry throne.

Every earth-dweller's face in fear was frozen,
all around the world saw it on their television,
yet the Witnesses had eyes only for heaven,
as they went up miraculously.
As they came so they went, in a cloud,
returning in full view of Antichrist and the world;
the reprobate fears fully justified immediately,
a great earthquake shook apart that great city.

No fear, only peace and joy on high,
while we in heaven looked on.
We also heard a call to dine,
the great marriage supper of the Lamb.
And while we go rejoicing to the feast,
the earth-dwellers have more cause to fear,
another vision seen in the heavens,
every inhabitant of an earth near uninhabitable,
the remnant of humankind and demons,
see the judgment inevitable,
unequivocally portrayed.

I, Saul, now Paul,
could see these things and all in all,
visions together of past, present and future,
was somewhat bemused even in my heavenly nature,
till my friend Ichabod, new-named Davek Cabhod,
(cleaving to the glory of God),
appeared, to explain fully,
how all these events coordinated
every aspect of God's plan from eternity,
until the words of God are fulfilled.

"The meaning of the visions and all that they
encompass is this," he said,
"First vision,
seen only in heaven,
the Judge, Son of Man, seen again on high
harvests the faithful, cloud-enthroned;
all who have died in his name
have now been taken up,
none died in vain.
But in the second vision,
which all in heaven and on earth can see,
another angel thrusts a sickle in,
a vision of condemnation for the damned,
judgment nigh;
the winepress will overflow with deep red blood,
a horse's bridle high."

Soon after the Bowls of Wrath pour out quickly:
sores for marked men, oceans turning bloody,
not one third but *all* the waters filthy.
In their thirst sun scorches with deadly fire,
but none repent, cursing God in reckless ire.

Sixth angel's bowl poured out, fierce wine,
Dragon, Beast and Prophet spew false spirits
all earth's armies summoned to destruction
at Armageddon, open shame, no garments,
naked, drunk, they stand before His wrath.
Noise, thunderings, lightnings, the earth
quakes as never before, signal the seventh,
the city splits in three, the nations' cities fall.
Babylon will fall, giant hailstones, and still
they blaspheme God and His tabernacle!

And Mystery, the great mother harlot, Babylon,
Antichurch who controlled corrupt rulers of the age,

who poured out, reveled in all her abomination,
who destroyed God's children in a bloody pillage,
is fated herself to destruction by her own.
The Beast's kings tear her limb from limb,
consumed with fire, desolate and naked,
God willed it, the words of God fulfilled,
the mystery of God is finished.
Her fall has been announced from age to age,
come out now, or share her every plague.

Davek Cabhod finished his explanation:
"While all this vast destruction on the earth
comes to completion,
here in heaven we are made ready,
not least in the marriage supper of the Lamb,
for we the bride are guaranteed victory,
when we return to Earth with the Lord of lords.
Pure and white are the linen garments
of the faithful entourage, the Bride,
not suitable to wear with stains
from the blood of bitter rebels,
when we attend His holy marriage supper.
So, this victory feast is set before the war,
no hubris this, for God has planned it all,
we may be absolutely sure,
His plan He will fulfill.

"While the earth-dwellers are called
in pain and destruction through bitter servitude,
knowing in their hearts
the Beast's doom and theirs,
we are called in anticipation of our victory,
in gladness with eternal life beckoning, longing,
in our hearts a constant cry,
for even greater service to our King."

13 THE MARRIAGE SUPPER

c. 2041 AD

A heavenly summons comes and Saul, now Paul, is led to his place at the table for the Marriage Supper of the Lamb. The events to follow become clear to him.

I, Paul, was now summoned personally,
each holy prophet, priest and king
summoned eternally, robed in white,
a holy angel to each one assigned,
if I had seen mine on the earth unveiled
I might, like John, have tried to worship.

But in that place and condition,
our body, mind and spirit
undergo a deep rendition,
the eyes of our head and heart,
incapable of such confusion.
He led me to the great table,
I made to take the lowest,
but grasping my arm firmly,
he led me to a higher seat.

And when all were seated,
the worship soon began,
spontaneously in that great multitude,
as our great King of kings again,
was heard to say in every heart,
"Well done, my good and faithful servant!"
It seemed many days
that we filled those halls with praise,
a delirium, though with clear mind and heart,
of joy and joyous expectation,

for our service to the King to start,
now and into eternity.

Then our Lord raised His cup on high,
and the bread,
spoke words of benediction,
consecration consummated,
I cannot fully translate them for you,
nor convey all their import,
full of light and glory as they were,
but they fully elaborated,
showed the true depth of meaning,
of His earthly declarations:
"I will no longer eat of it
until it is fulfilled,
in the kingdom of God,
nor drink of the fruit of the vine
until that kingdom come.
You, my brothers and friends,
proclaimed my death till I came,
now I am come and you will share
everlasting blessing and authority,
in My eternal dominion."

A mighty shout of joyous pure fulfillment,
shook the heavens there
as all the angels above, below
and all surrounding,
joined in the chorus of delight and celebration,
the feast went on it seemed for seven years,
though on old earth events
drew quickly to their conclusion.

And though we knew these celebrations
would recur many times,
the call to other purpose,

came too soon it seemed,
but all instantly obeyed.
"The marriage supper is complete,
the bride for war must be made ready!"
Each of us robed in white linen,
our full and sufficient armour,
each on a white horse, set as victor,
there is one outcome only,
victory, to the holy and pure.

He refines like launderer's soap
and so will we,
for the unclean Beast and his slaves
there is no hope.
Everyone in the host heard him say,
"They do not fear me aright,
consider my grace and patient mercy
as the Lamb of God,
to be weakness, presumptuously.
Soon enough they will know me,
as the Lion of Judah,
and the sword of my mouth,
an iron rod to batter faithless shields
and helmets of damnation,"
so said the Lord of Hosts.
And I, along with every other heavenly warrior,
resolved to cast down every opposition,
every foul thing, high or lower,
that sets itself against God's power,
hating His Christ and every Christian.

Now hear the seventh trump sound,
the bowls poured out,
the harlot judged,
the saints rise with a shout,
the Amen has been uttered,

the Hallelujah called,
the saints for battle all well-armed,
every one a warrior of light riding forth,
perfect time, perfect formation,
even as their captain,
with sword and rod of iron,
who leads us at Armageddon.

14 ARMAGEDDON

c. 2041 AD

Shortly after the Bowl Judgments, only days or weeks at most in earth time, the battles of the Armageddon war are intense but one-sided. Satan's vast hordes are overwhelmed, Christ personally raises the siege at Bozrah, the Antichrist and False Prophet are captured in a last stand at Jerusalem. The King of kings takes His judgment seat in the Valley of Jehoshaphat and judges first the spiritual enemies, Antichrist and False Prophet; then He and his followers declare judgments on the surviving earth-dwellers and their nations. Last of all, Satan himself is sentenced to a thousand years exile in the Abyss.

So, timely, the King returns in power
on a white horse, faithful and true,
righteous judge and maker of war,
a name written that no one knew.
His robe dipped in blood, the Word of God,
God's armies linen-clothed, His mouth a sword,
He, the King of kings, of all lords the Lord.
The carrion birds are summoned to a feast,
the flesh of all His foes, both small and great.

Pay extremely close attention,
you who hear or read these words,
the prophecy is not for those
who lose the final war in time to come,
reprobate earth-dwellers,
but you, now in this moment of time,
hear and come out from Babylon this very hour.
Learn to obey the gospel of our Lord,
before He vengeance takes in flaming fire
and you destroyed by the glory of His power.
His feet will stand soon enough on Olivet,

and every saint will stand with Him on it.
The year of God's redeemed has comfort in these days,
so, cast that old life behind your back, look to the future,
turn away from empty loves and false passions,
become a child of God in humble surrender
to Him who died for you on that cross.
Your reward guaranteed and incalculable,
even on the New Earth in the making,
for all His faithful children in the New Jerusalem
will drink deeply the consolation of her bosom.

Do not be like those stiff-necked,
hard-hearted earth-dwellers,
knowing their doom but still stubbornly refusing
to admit their crimes and sins of idol worship,
clinging to their allegiance to the Beast,
by the False Prophet, deceived yet self-deceived.
They think by force of arms they can resist
the power of heaven which even the Dragon
could not for a moment oppose;
each time he overstepped the mark, cast down.

"Some of us arrayed for the battles,"
said Paul, directly to us, Jon and Sarah,
"had not thought in our former lives
that we would physically fight,
not indeed the Lord Himself;
but we soon discovered that
in the end evil must be confronted,
it ever believes presumptuously
that the good will yield, intimidated,
daring not to face them down courageously.
Yet in Christ we have discernment and discrimination,
know when to turn the cheek,
in hope of a conversion,
and when to strike a blow for deliverance,
the righteous anger of the meek."

In that grim but joyous hour the choice was clear,
no demon or earth-dweller could come to salvation,
their choice made and set in stony heart,
all that remained was for us to do our part.
So, vast armies will avail them nothing from His ire,
nor ours,
Beast and False Prophet, the seditious pair,
will be cast alive into the brimstone lake of fire,
their followers will die by the rider's sword and iron rod,
and ours,
a faithful judgment feast for every bird.

The Plain of Jezreel was packed closer,
than any assembly ever on the earth,
no room to run, no time for second thought.
Like the reaping of a combine harvester,
the agents of heaven swept through the assembled masses,
the earth-dwellers as Satan and his minions
planned all along,
mere cannon fodder for his ambitious nihilism.

They fall by the thousand,
to sleep the sleep of death till judgment day,
their destruction by the saints whom they destroyed,
fitting, as the holy sing a song of battle joy.

And their Lord did not forget those at Bozrah,
the battle on the fields nearly over,
departs by Himself to free the protected there.
And when they see Him arrayed in all His power,
soon dispatching all surrounding enemies,
all praise and worship, fall on their faces,
this is the true Messiah's hour.
Last to come, in this age, into the kingdom,
joy mingled with sadness,
and grief for errors past,

humble themselves before the King of kings,
acknowledge Yeshua ha Mashiach,
their Lord of lords, at last!

So they follow Him, up to Jerusalem,
stand with Christ in all His power,
and I, Paul, proudly stood with Him,
on the Mount of Olives already riven,
saw the Holy City occupied by fear,
enclosed by the last army of the Antichrist.
Yet light still shone from the sanctuary,
which the Two Witnesses made clean,
where I had died,
Antichrist had not dared to approach again,
and the earth shook from the armies of the Lord.

And as He stood there on the riven Olivet,
Messiah wept tears of pure joy, this time,
said, "Now you know the things this day
that make for peace, in me,
Messiah and Lord.
Your eyes are opened,
the wall soon broken down."

So, the host of the regenerate invade,
overtake the city at every compass point,
advancing in close ranks, none could resist,
running up and along the walls,
through every window we leaped,
supernatural strength in resurrection bodies,
soon fallen or captured, all our enemies.

False Christ and False Prophet captured last,
hiding in a cracked cistern void of water,
and I, Paul, among those who discovered them,
said, "Now, you are forsaken, now desolate,

you who became abomination of desolation,
whose destination is the Lake of Fire."
They, dragged in fear, though still defiant,
even before the great Lord of All,
seated on a judgment seat,
over the Valley of Jehoshaphat,
every saint had access there,
their judgment inevitable but fair,
the wicked pair were, in despair,
cast before the time into the Lake of Fire.

And as Jerusalem was cleansed, now forever,
to become the millennial seat of global power,
the nations who survived the calamity
of plagues and the Armageddon wars,
were judged by faithful Jew and Gentile righteously,
and new rulers from the elect as kings and queens,
appointed over every city and all nations.

But last to be judged in this tribunal holy,
the ancient enemy of God and Man,
Satan dragged cursing, still full of blasphemy,
even now, maligning God's creation,
the product of his own malediction.

15 MILLENNIUM AND JUDGMENT

c. 2042–3042 AD/Mill.1–1000

A New Calendar Begins

The evidence overwhelming,
the history of heaven,
and the human race, the accuser's condemnation,
his mouth was stopped, no blasphemy permitted,
though he clearly still persisted,
in craving destruction
of all God had created.

So, the old serpent is bound down in chains,
Satan laid so low in dishonor,
bound for a thousand years in the Abyss,
key turned, no more to play deceiver nor accuser.
Judgment ongoing is given to those upon the thrones,
no mark of beast upon their heads or hands,
living and reigning with Christ a thousand years.
Blessed and holy those in the first resurrection,
priests of God and Christ in the last millennium.

A thousand years may seem but a day in heaven,
from God and every angel
and each regenerated saint's perspective,
yet still a fruitful time for the saints,
who would share in Christ's eternal dominion.
The renewal and restoration of the old earth,
a seemingly impossible and pointless mission,
(as some have said)
not impossible at all when the King is on his throne,
fulfilling all His purpose on this afflicted planet
to bring many more souls to that new birth.

For many unregenerate survived the wars,
old and young who came out of tribulation,
unfit for battle on the plains of Armageddon,
many had rejected the great deception
but failed to believe in Christ,
now every false hope of Antichrist,
and he himself cast to destruction.

Seeing Christ in glory,
every earth-dweller takes the knee,
they must live normal lives on earth,
over forty generations,
suffer the cycle of birth and death
with the immortal saints among them.
The saints will rule with the King's commission,
training for their even greater destiny,
eternal dominion,
in new earth and new heaven,
the King of king's priority command and desire,
in the old earth's last millennium,

"Be my salt and be my leaven,
snatch many times a million
from the eternal fire for salvation."

And so, a thousand years of peace began,
the perfect rule of the Lord of lords,
the earth soon began to blossom once again.
Directed by the saints the once earth-dwellers,
within a generation,
found purpose and new hope in life
unfettered by demonic accusation.
Yet though Satan was bound,
the seeds he had planted,
in the sinful nature of the unredeemed,
led many to resent and question

the nature and justice of their condition.
Though they dared no open opposition,
to the manifest goodness of his global reign,
many stored and nourished bitter seeds of doubt,
conveyed to their children
in the next generation.

The task of the saints at first seemed easy:
to lead all who had survived directly to the Lord.
Yet time proved a bitter enemy,
not for them who immortal lived,
but for those they served who had but a short span.
Some of the elect were set in fixed positions,
rulers under Christ to maintain peace and build,
others had more roving, Spirit-led commissions,
as I, Paul, was given,
to touch many lives, lead many back to God.

"And so, Sarah and Jon," Paul concluded,
"we come to our present condition;
the millennium has begun
and you must choose your own direction.
You have the rest of your life to choose,
but give me a little more time,
to show you what lies beyond this frame,
to put your choices in perspective,
and make them, by God's grace,
eternally effective.

"A thousand years will go unimpaired,
this old earth will be repaired and prepared.
Your hope and expectation
is not so different from mine
when I was in your position,
though the Lord is here and manifest now.
There will still be a time of tribulation,

a time of rebellion and judgment,
God's and our great enemy
seemingly ascendant,
yet all the ultimate conclusion,
God's summation of all history.
The Gog-Magog war to come
will be a mere footnote,
in which we will not fight.
God Himself will cast them down,
the Great White Throne decisive for eternity,
the end of all eschatology.

"You have seen the work begun,
for its ultimate transition,
a God-destined consummation,
not just a new Earth but a new Heaven.

"So, when the thousand years expire,
the age-old hater, Satan, will deceive again,
you will not be here but your descendants will,
let all your choices now bless that future generation.

"Mystery of deception, to battle they will be gathered,
Gog-Magog, many from every nation harried,
one thousand years of light not enough for all,
the reprobate prefer darkness though in thrall,
till fire comes from heaven in great hail.
The adversary cast at last into the lake of fire,
tormented day and night forevermore."

I, Sarah, with softened heart interrupted once again,
"Paul, and I think Jon has a similar question,
about the judgments of the lake of fire so far,
we know the Antichrist and False Prophet were
already thrown in after Armageddon,
and now it seems that after this millennium,

Satan himself will be cast down to join them.
We know from Scripture, and all your teaching,
what comes after the Gog-Magog uprising,
the Great White Throne judgment,
the final state of all deciding.
The lake of fire seems that last judgment,
for the reprobate,
it almost seems the false trinity
of Devil, Antichrist and his prophet,
are punished prematurely,
before their actual judgment.
We know God is entirely just,
perhaps the answer is in the question.
So what is the nature of their judgment,
judgment richly deserved by them?"

Paul looked lovingly upon me, eyes clear,
responded, "I see your faithful heart,
quick to uphold our God's true nature,
his perfect justice, nothing in his polity unjust,
faithful and loving, ever pure.
The answer as I understand is this,
(though I, immortal, am still learning,
in this time of service)
two types of creatures are cast into the fire,
once-were-angels in heaven who rebelled,
and humans whose names are not written,
in the Book of Life.
It is not difficult to understand,
that angels were judged previously,
their eternal destruction merely delayed,
while God's purpose worked out
in all the rest of His creation.
The demons need not face the Great White Throne,
because they are already in their just position,
judged fit for eternal fire when cast down,

both at creation and the abomination of desolation.
Only human beings
are judged at the Great White Throne.
So why, you ask, are the Beast and his prophet
seeming prematurely cast in?
The answer can be deduced
from the nature of their works,
and their constant, importunate blasphemies;
they had surrendered their souls to the Satan,
the Beast particularly to the spirit of Abaddon.
With demons they consorted and engaged,
to such a vile degree they became
fully identified, by the evil spirits consumed,
not merely deceived,
they have become deception,
and so, they share the judgment already given,
against every hell-spawn spirit cast from heaven.
The only loose end seems to be,
concerning Death and Hades' final end,
but they had charge of every reprobate human soul,
they could not end until their end decreed."

We, Jon and Sarah nod in silent affirmation,
this wisdom seemed to answer
our questions on divine retribution,
and Paul continued:
"So comes the great harvest and separation
saints and sinners whole must judgment face
stand naked and alone at the Great White Throne
Book of Works and the Book of Life in place.
Did you give me food when I was hungry
or give me drink when I was thirsty?
Welcomed me, a naked stranger, clothed me?
Depart to punishment eternal or eternal life
as you may or may not be the Groom's good wife."

And Paul added a final, personal point,
to strengthen us in hope:
"You have been tempted to sin,
because you compared yourselves to me,
ungraciously,
assuming I was superior to you in God's eyes,
but truly the gap between us is miniscule,
compared to our Lord.
Just as before the millennium all saints
were merely sinners saved by grace,
of high or low degree in men's eyes
it mattered not, all equal before his face.

"So, I, Paul, and all those like me,
and they are many,
remember clearly what we were,
reminded constantly
by the wounds of Jesus Christ.
Yet we, like you, remember,
in joy and love entire,
those wounds he suffered so that we
might be healed of our own, self-inflicted,
and those of our enemy.
I, Paul, am simply further along the path of healing;
whether started earlier or not
it matters not in the infinity of time,
yet I still learn and grow in Him.
This millennium is yet another ground of proving,
as we grow into his image of perfection.
'Be perfect as my heavenly Father is,' he said,
and so, you and I will grow toward
the light of his beauty.
"Into eternity, to holy work subjected,
co-creators with Him
in unimaginable reality.
This millennium is just a beginning,

the last era of salvation,
for you and all your descendants
to become what God meant you to be:
mighty overcomers, warriors in his name,
victors over sin and death,
by the power of His name.
And so will we all go,
into eternity, new creation
in a new Jerusalem,
blessed, united wholly in love,
with Him and each other,
saved, sanctified, perfected
as firstfruits to His glory."

He paused to see if this was too much for us,
we glanced but a moment at each other,
our eyes met and knew that we were one,
fully sensed each other's heart rhythm,
united in our soul revelation,
a knowing which doubt could no longer smother.
We, Jon and Sarah said, with shining eyes,
"Speak on, sweet Paul,
we are now of one mind with you, in Him.
The love of our Lord,
you have taught and modelled well,
in full assurance now we trust
Him who is the All in All.
We have chosen Christ, salvation and redemption,
look forward to the path of sanctification,
completed at our resurrection;
seeing this lesser life now in such perspective,
we choose life.
But tell us more and teach us truly,
you have given a glimpse of eternity,
but now we know there is even more to come,
a triumph to infinity."

Paul, responded,
"Dear hearts, I will, with great joy, do so,
for now, I see your hearts are free at last,
you have full faith which will see a great reward,
at the Great White Throne,
accompanied by every following generation,
a constant legacy for all your children,
and your children's children.
It will seem a mere step in time,
at the end of this millennium,
when immortal you become,
worthy of the praise of the Lamb."

16 ETERNAL DOMINION

Paul elaborates for Jon and Sarah on the eternal implications of everything that has led up to the millennial era.

Paul continued his peroration,
"In truth, our salvation and regeneration,
even my service in this millennium,
are only the beginning of our true lives,
lived in the light of the holy city,
in glorious servitude to Him,
the One who gives true freedom.

"Death and Hades will be in the Lake of Fire,
time for a New Heaven and New Earth,
first heaven and earth and even sea expire,
as the New Jerusalem descends in a new birth.
Not the flood which covered all the world,
but with fervent heat the elements will unfold,
creation beginning anew in shining gold.
Behold, the destruction of all liars, every coward,
all enemies only prepared the way for the bride.

"Holy Jerusalem, the great city, will descend out of heaven,
Light of precious stones, God's glory, clear as crystal,
twelve tribes and twelve apostles, the One New Man,
inscribed on the gates and foundations of the wall.
Pearls carved for gates, streets like gold transparent,
all precious stones comprise its fundament.
No need for sun and moon, the Lamb its light,
the pure river, water of life proceeding
from His throne,
no more curse, leaves of healing,
for all He calls His own.

"Then we will see perfection of creation
full attained;
we will walk in many a garden
with our great friend,
eat from trees of knowledge and of life,
paradise renewed,
a life of worship, service, and love,
world without end."

17 EPILOGUE

The Lord God of the holy prophets has spoken,
read and absorb his word in revelation,
keep the words of His prophecy, worship Him
He is Alpha and Omega, Beginning and End,
prophecy unsealed, gone is the enemy's time.
Let him who thirsts take the water of life freely,
be not of those who love and practice the lie.
He testifies and says, "Surely, I come quickly."
Believe the Word, don't take from or add to it,
Amen, even so, Come, Lord Jesus Christ!

Appendices

Appendix A outlines the Scripture-derived narrative of the last days which the preceding poem is based on; Appendix B provides a brief rationale for that narrative. The latter is based on a full analysis of all the scriptures relevant to the last-days narrative, based in turn on a synopsis of all those scriptures.

APPENDIX A

The Narrative Overview

The first segment of time in the chronological narrative is the *Beginning of Birth Pains*. This covers all of the history of the church from Pentecost until the present time. The gospels, and the early chapters of Revelation particularly, *foreshadow*[1] the events of this long era. Deception and false teaching constantly afflict the church, and war and natural disasters were often blamed on the early Christians for their provocative 'offence to the gods.'

The time that follows the nearly two millennia of the Beginning of Birth Pains is designated the *Difficult Labour*. This represents an *intensification*[2] and *globalisation* of what has gone before. Christians are persecuted and killed in greater numbers, many apostasise from the faith; only a select few (relatively speaking) continue to stand on the biblical gospel. One way or another, the gospel has been made freely available to the whole world by this time. We may soon enter, or have already entered, this phase.

The antichristian and antisemitic attacks by the pagan blood and soil fascists of Nazi Germany and similar extremes of atheistic communism in the twentieth century at least foreshadow such a time. The merging of extreme leftist ideologies and Islamic fundamentalism in various forms since WW2, the formation of ISIS, and the beginning of the destruction of the Middle Eastern churches at the turn of the millennium, could indicate that such a time is nearly upon us.

1. The use of the word *foreshadow* generally means that events described in earlier prophecies, which have full or partial fulfilments in an historical time frame, also indicate events which will unfold in the future, and they point to one final catastrophic time.

2. *Intensification* is an important theme since it represents the linear nature of the sequence of events through the several judgments of the very last days.

During the period of the Difficult Labour and before the hidden rapture,[3] a charismatic and popular new world leader will begin to emerge. He will later develop great economic, political and military influence. There is no unequivocal biblical indication of how long the Difficult Labour will last, only the certainty that it is just a beginning, a precursor. The Difficult Labour is *not* the Seal judgment time. However, two things happen at the end of this period of time, one of which constitutes a clear marker that this time is over and the time of the Great Tribulation and its precursors, the time of God's final judgments, is close.

The first event, though not perceived on earth, is described in Revelation 4 and 5. God, in *the Throne Room of Heaven,* prepares the way for the events which will follow. The Lamb of God, who alone in the royal court is worthy to open it, takes the scroll which authorises and sets in motion the Seal judgments to follow. This is the beginning of the just war to end all just wars. His Lordship is proclaimed in heaven, foreshadowing what is to come on earth when he returns in glory as the King of kings.

The clear marker, the first fruit of this action, is a harvest of the saints on earth who remain true to him. This has been designated the *Hidden Rapture* of the elect saints, since Christ remains hidden from the world in it. It has a political aspect in that it is like the evacuation of nationals from a foreign power just before war is declared against it. Another aspect is that of judgment, because it marks a differentiation among those calling themselves Christian. True believers are taken up and the false or backslidden left behind.

Following the Hidden Rapture, a defining event, or series of events, will be the emergence of *144,000* Messianic Christian leaders, Jews who have a deep knowledge of both OT and NT Scripture and who had been on the verge of a commitment to faith in Yeshua

3. Some still assert that *rapture* is not a biblical word. This is a dated argument which is easily proved false. The Greek word *harpadzo* is used in 1 Thess 4:17; Matt 11:12; Acts 8:39; 1 Cor 12:2, 4; and Rev 12:5 and means to be *caught up* or *away* or *taken by force*, all of which are applicable. The word rapture in English comes from the Latin Vulgate Bible verbal equivalent, *rapiemur*, of which *raptus* is the noun.

ha Mashiach[4] but had not yet done so. The disappearance of millions, or at least hundreds of thousands of Gentile Christians and a sizeable number of believing Jews, and the later emergence of a significant believing Jewish bloc cannot be ignored by the apostate, lukewarm church, many of whom will understand its significance and soon repent. They will either turn back to God or turn to him for the first time.

Some, of course, will also double down, hardening even further. The non-Christian world will also take note, but no doubt will try to explain it away. However, depending on the numbers taken, the Hidden Rapture will be easier or harder for the authorities to explain away. Many, of course, will close their ears to any biblical explanation, and the fact that many superficially professing Christians are left behind will give them some grounds for such wilful deafness.

The nature of the Hidden Rapture will also be significant. If, as in the *Left Behind* movies, every young child is taken then social disruption would be catastrophic. Even if, as I suspect, only the children of believers are taken (as well as children who had made an independent personal commitment to Christ), social unrest would still be considerable and the event require some sort of explanation by the authorities. Many people will find the no-doubt facile, non-biblical explanations hard to swallow and begin to investigate the faith. The implication is that the years of the Seal judgments after the Hidden Rapture will be a time of unprecedented revival. The duration of the Seal judgments up until the defining event of the Antichrist's desecration of a rebuilt temple[5] is uncertain scripturally, but will probably be between three and seven years in length.

4. This Jewish phrase for *Jesus Christ* is used occasionally to emphasise his Jewishness in the context in which it appears.

5. Arguments exist for and against a rebuilding of a third, last-days Jewish Temple. Many say it is not possible, since Christ's sacrifice replaced the temple sacrifices, so there would be no purpose for it in God's plan. In this view, if such a temple was built, it would have no significance, being built in unbelief (in Christ).

However, it is undeniable that there are hopes and plans to build such a temple, and that the political situation could change to enable it, so we must

After the Hidden Rapture and the following disorder, a new world leader will emerge as a stabilising force—he will become known to Christian believers as the Antichrist. He will have a radical agenda which will be accepted by many as the price of peace and prosperity. Many Jews may identify him as the Messiah and Muslims as the Mahdi. Progress and order will seem to emerge from the chaos associated with the Hidden Rapture in the first years of the Seal judgments, which I have called the *Minor Tribulation*, a kind of prelude to the Great Tribulation. This will be a time of great disruption as the *Seal Judgments begin*, quite possibly involving a third world war and an increasing, but not yet state-sponsored, persecution of Christians. If a worldwide war does occur it will probably be of short duration. In the relative progress and order that eventually emerge the Antichrist will take the credit and initiate major changes as part of his peace plan. The third temple will be built, and there may be straws in the wind indicating this possibility even before the Hidden Rapture. A standard, probably electronically based global currency and means of exchange (controlled by personal and group identification) will be initiated. The Social Credit system in China probably foreshadows this. These will eventually be administered by a global system with religious, cultural and economic power, but also with political influence. The Bible calls this *Babylon* and it is effectively the *Antichurch* of the Antichrist. Babylon will have one primary administrative centre, like a world capital, but with six subsidiary centres through which the Babylonian administration will operate around the world. Babylon will have a powerful religious core, presumably

---

consider the temple as a potential reality. Specific arguments will be made in the course of the discussion, but generally we may say that from a Christian point of view, there would indeed be no salvific purpose in building the temple—the sacrifices are defunct. However, the original temples were the place of God's dwelling with his people, as well as of sacrifices. God appears to have a last-days purpose in a third Temple, at the very least as a prefiguring of His ultimate location with us in the New Jerusalem, in the New Heaven and Earth, where His immediate presence dwells physically among us, replacing the temple. Christ occupying the temple during His millennial rule would prefigure that final state, preparing the way for His and our Eternal Dominion. Such a temple would be both memorial and promise.

made up of representatives from all the major religions. They will effectively become traitors to the one true God they supposedly serve, so the title *Whore of Babylon* seems appropriate. Scripture says that they will kill true believers in God's name: "the time is coming that whoever kills you will think that he offers God service" (John 16:2).

The same lawlessness that we see emerging on the left today will continue to develop, but on the right as well (there will be few remaining in the political centre). The renewed church which emerges almost immediately after the Hidden Rapture will become a major target of most if not all political and state-sponsored religious groups. Increasing social pressure to conform to the new world leader's seemingly reasonable demands will only increase and will culminate in active persecution and deaths in some places. For those who do conform it will be a period of seeming progress, prosperity and peace, much like Hitler's Germany in the mid- to late-1930s. Marginalised groups, especially believing Christians and Jews, will receive little support when they are openly discriminated against and persecuted.

However, the true church will grow exponentially in numbers on the back of the persecution, galvanised by the Hidden Rapture and the clear last-days marker of the third temple. There is no clear marker for when the temple will be built, but it must be after the Hidden Rapture and at least three-and-a-half years before its desecration by the Antichrist. There are no clear markers for the timing of this period after the Hidden Rapture up until the desecration of the temple. But because the seven-year peace period is broken halfway through there must be time to reach a peace agreement and build the temple. So there will be an indeterminate time after the Hidden Rapture until the peace agreement is made and the temple is built, then three-and-a-half years after the dedication of the temple until the abomination of desolation which desecrates it and breaks the peace agreement.

Religious structures will remain in place as compliant leaders pledge themselves to the Antichrist's agenda, just as many church leaders did to the Nazi agenda in the 1930s and 1940s. An antichrist-like figure called the False Prophet will also emerge as the Antichrist's mouthpiece and will exercise authority and spiritual powers on his behalf. The False Prophet will presumably have control over the administrative system called Babylon, but will not identify with it.

Some years after the Hidden Rapture everything changes suddenly with open war against the tribulation saints during the latter three-and-a-half years of the Seal judgments. This is the beginning of the first three-and-a-half years of the *Great Tribulation.* It will begin with the Antichrist desecrating the temple, probably with an image of himself—the *Abomination of Desolation.* People will be required to worship it or at least pledge their allegiance and this pattern may be repeated in key locations all around the world. This will be marked by the *Flight of Jewish People* from Israel, and from Jerusalem in particular. The Antichrist will carry out a Holocaust-style purge of Jewish people from Jerusalem (at least) and probably all Israel. The surviving mainly orthodox Jews will flee to a place prepared for them, probably in the Bozrah region, where they will be supernaturally protected. This is when the Mount of Olives is split to enable their escape from the encircling armies of the Antichrist who sought to trap and exterminate them. Presumably the Antichrist's motive is to prevent the mass conversion of the Jewish people in the near future, trying to undercut one of the key prophetic elements of the Lord's plan in the last days. Most Messianic believers will have left Israel earlier, having been forewarned, as they were prior to the Roman destruction. Believers everywhere will have to shelter from the storm, and will no doubt have earlier formed cooperative enterprises which can operate independently of the world economic system.

The first half of the seven-year Great Tribulation period (the latter half of the Seal judgments) will be intense for the believers who emerged during the years after the Hidden Rapture (the period of the early Seal judgments). The period of the latter Seal judgments, the first three-and-a-half years of the Great Tribulation, will be a time of even more intense suffering and persecution of the true church, as the Seal judgments play out and the

Antichrist attacks the true church directly. However, the abomination that causes desolation is an act of blasphemy too far by Satan and precipitates *War in Heaven,* as a result of which Satan and his forces are permanently cast down to the earth. They will literally bring hell on earth during the Great Tribulation.

Unrestrained state-sanctioned lawlessness (like the nineteenth century Russian pogroms instigated by the Tsar) and its accompanying madness, will result in the deaths of many Christians and believing Jews, generally by beheading, which has already become a hallmark of some radical terrorist groups today. Some believers will actively resist with physical force, but most will have been disempowered and will eschew physical violence anyway. Concomitant with all these events will be the rise of the *False Prophet,* who supports the *False Christ,* the Antichrist, and many kindred spirits who will maintain the deceptions of the Antichrist and False Prophet and try to prevent conversions to Christ. The Antichrist and False Prophet, described in Rev. 13, are the epitome of the general types of false christs and false prophets mentioned in the gospels and epistles.

Jesus' Return Enthroned in the Clouds will mark the end of the suffering for the first group of tribulation saints: they will be raptured openly from the farthest parts of earth to join those from the farthest parts of heaven who have been martyred and already raptured. These are the saints who repented after the Hidden Rapture over seven years previously, and their converts. The spectacular sign of the Son of Man followed by the open return of Jesus Christ enthroned in the clouds signals the midpoint of the Great Tribulation. Up to this time Satan and his followers have had more or less free rein to oppress the saints, and to prepare to resist the doom that they know is coming.

The fact that Jesus' return at this time is described as His being enthroned on a cloud seems to imply that He remains there for a time while some of the eschatological events play out, especially the ministry of the Two Witnesses sent by Him to testify.

So, counterintuitively, Jesus' open advent in the clouds does not immediately halt the troubles on earth, although the saints still living at that time will be taken up and away from earth's problems in the *Open Rapture of the Saints.* Unlike the Hidden Rapture of the saints, this time the differentiation will primarily be between believers and nonbelievers. This clear separation, however it occurs, means that during the Trumpet judgments, after Jesus' open revelation of himself enthroned in the clouds and the open rapture of the Seal judgment saints, many *earth-dwellers*[6] will reject their allegiance to the Antichrist and his system.

As after the Hidden Rapture, another global revival will occur, perhaps eclipsing the earlier one proportionately (the world's population will be somewhat reduced at this stage). There will be a powerful Jewish flavour to this revival, indeed most Jews will be part of it,[7] since the appearance of the sign of the Son of Man (presumably, the cross) and Jesus' actual appearance enthroned in the clouds will be unequivocal for most. Many Gentiles will also convert although, with the mass conversion of the Jews, this will be the end or at least the beginning of the end, of the *Times of the Gentiles.* Of course, the Antichrist and his allies will not be pleased as this revival will significantly weaken their power and pose a direct threat to their rule. Not only will the rebellion of the new saints threaten them, but also a new force for leadership in the world arises, the *Two Witnesses.* The Two Witnesses will cleanse the Temple and also be a confirmatory sign to many Jews that Jesus, not the Antichrist, is the true Messiah.

The time is not yet ripe for Jesus' final assault on the Antichrist's global kingdom because more people can be brought to repentance and into His kingdom. So, he commissions the Two Witnesses as plenipotentiary ambassadors to lead the new saints on earth, the Jewish ones especially, in their resistance to the Antichrist. This may be the time when the Antichrist is mortally

6. *Earth-dwellers* is a term used in Revelation to describe those who remain on earth and persistently deny the gospel and persecute the saints.

7. However, the unbelieving Jews who earlier escaped to Bozrah will be those very Orthodox who cannot accept Jesus as Messiah until he fulfils the final prophecy: his appearance as the victorious conqueror. That will happen in the final phase of the Parousia at Armageddon and Bozrah, and they will at last acknowledge him as Lord and Savior ('and so all Israel will be saved' Rom 11:26).

wounded (by the Two Witnesses) and then 'miraculously' raised in a last-ditch attempt to turn the deceived masses against the true Messiah who has appeared in the heavens. This raising from the dead could in fact be a zombie-like reactivation of the Antichrist. He would be reactivated by Apollyon, the spirit from the Abyss, perhaps through the medium of the False Prophet.

However, many new saints will come to faith because of the Two Witnesses' gospel message, as well as the fact that they are able to challenge the Antichrist successfully. The Witnesses carry out their ministry from the Temple and its precincts, though the Antichrist will still control the outer courts and Jerusalem. These ambassadors have the power of God at their disposal, effectively the power of the *Trumpet Judgments,* so they will weaken the Antichrist's influence and power considerably.

The three-and-a-half-year course of the Trumpet Judgments (with their destruction of one third of all things) is the last opportunity for repentance in this age. The Antichrist and False Prophet will initiate all-out war against believers and the Two Witnesses, which will eventually result in a *Pyrrhic Victory of the Enemy over the Saints and the Two Witnesses.* It is a pyrrhic victory because

a. it is simply permitted by God, and
b. after the horrific total destruction of the *Bowl Judgments,* all of those martyred saints will return with many others in the army of the victorious King of kings.

The world is given a visible token of their return when the Two Witnesses are openly raptured before the eyes of the earth-dwellers who, nonetheless, do not repent.

The Judgment of the Harlot Babylon, the world system which supported the Antichrist, occurs during the Bowl Judgments, largely at the hands of the Antichrist's 10 kings (though at God's instigation), who resented her power and control over them.

The armies of heaven, led by the *Returning King of kings, the Rider on the White Horse,* will then destroy the Antichrist forces at *Armageddon* and *Bozrah.* It is at Bozrah where the Lord will personally fight to deliver an unbelieving remnant of the Jewish people from a siege. With this final regal manifestation of the Lord all of them believe at last. These late believers will live out normal lives during the millennium, unless they are sovereignly, belatedly, given new resurrection bodies. This is because the *Marriage Supper of the Lamb* occurs just before the battle, not after it as one might expect. Because the victory is so certain, the marriage—which is also a victory feast—is held before the battle, not after.

After the battle at Bozrah the Lord comes up to Jerusalem where he stands on the Mount of Olives to reverse the message of Matt 23:37–39 and Luke 13:34–35. Jerusalem is retaken, the temple cleansed (or perhaps destroyed and rebuilt), and God's enemies are judged in the Valley of Jehoshaphat, a judgment partly carried out by the saints: the *Antichrist and False Prophet are Consigned to the Lake of Fire* and *Satan is Locked Away in the Abyss.*

Christ's Millennial Reign from Jerusalem follows, with the *Saints Exercising Authority* on his behalf over the unsaved left alive around the world. The resurrected saints (those martyred during the Trumpet judgments at least,[8] and presumably those raised earlier by rapture) remain, undying in their new, regenerated bodies, for the millennium. But the surviving unconverted and those who come late to faith in the millennial age live normal lifespans. The authority of the saints to rule and judge will evidently be 'to the Jew first, and then the Gentile.' Under Christ's kingship Jewish leaders will rule in Israel and probably occupy the significant regional and national leaderships around the world. Gentile leaders will rule under their authority in the natural order of things. Two significant purposes for the period of the millennium might be (a) further conversions of unbelievers, the last to do so, and (b) the refining and perfecting of the saints in exercising heavenly authority, often in difficult circumstances since the world is not yet perfect. This training equips them for the *Eternal Dominion* of the New Heaven and New Earth, which is, of course, the ultimate manifestation of the Kingdom of God.

During the millennium Jerusalem is established as the capital of the world, with the King of kings reigning either from a cleansed,

8. Rev 20:4–6

renewed third temple—which is most likely (Dan 8:14)—or a fourth temple built entirely by Messiah himself. All nations send representatives to the covenant feast celebrations, though probably without the animal sacrifices. After the thousand years Satan is released, deceives many of the unconverted, and tries to attack Jerusalem with the *Gog-Magog Alliance.* God destroys them all without using his army and the *Great White Throne Judgment* follows, which is followed in turn by the creation of a *New Heaven and a New Earth* and the descent of the *New Jerusalem.*

It is important to note that our existence then will not be in some ethereal, non-bodily state in an amorphous heaven. Rather, in our renewed bodies, which in their perfection will have many properties beyond our present weakness, we will carry out the work we are destined for on the New Earth but will have free commerce between the New Heaven and the New Earth. At this stage it seems likely that all believers become renewed or confirmed in a sinless state that cannot be broken—we will be more than Adam and Eve in innocence, we will be incapable of sin. Their created bodies had the potential for immortal life, ours will be filled with it. Holiness will be truly established for eternity in the *Eternal Dominion* of God and the saints.

This narrative, when looked at carefully, is very consistent and coherent with the relatively fragmented biblical narrative of the last days, but there is a rationale for the timing and sequence of events in this narrative which is equally consistent and coherent.

APPENDIX B

The Rationale for the Timing and Sequence of the Last-Days Events

The whole sequence described in the narrative overview is established by the following scriptural rationale:

- The requirement for full imminence of the Lord's parousia—or, in this study, its first phase—means a hidden rapture before the significant events of the end times begin is essential to maintain that imminence. Markers like the rebuilding of the third temple or the seven-year peace treaty cannot have substance until then, since they are part of specific time frames and would permit calculation of various sorts based on the biblical data. Even so, no one will know the precise day or hour of any of the phases of the parousia, even the latter ones.
- Although there is no certain timing for the period which we have called the minor tribulation, such a time must follow the hidden rapture,[1] since certain events must occur and come to fruition before the seven-year peace agreement. The Antichrist must become established, largely through a manipulation of war and peace-making; a provisional world government at least must be mapped out; the temple planned

1. Some Christian understandings (e.g., the 'pre-Wrath' mid tribulation position) fail to see the opening of the Seals as a revelation of judgments, partly on the basis that the fifth seal refers to the persecution of the saints, not judgment. This seems a very superficial treatment of the obvious meaning of the texts about the consequences of the opening of the Seals and the results. Those who advocate a pre-wrath, midtribulation rapture theory are forced to say that the Seal judgments are not the time of God's wrath (which is, rather, the Trumpet and Bowl judgments) but the wrath of Satan or the Antichrist. They say that the first Seal judgments are simply the same as the events of Matt 24:4–7, the beginning of birth pains. However, since it is Christ who opens all the Seals, it cannot be said that they represent the wrath of Satan or Antichrist: they must be God's judgment. In any case, as we show later, the saints suffering this wrath are those saved after the hidden rapture, not church-age saints.

and the terms of the peace agreement worked out. The time frame for the minor tribulation must be three-and-a-half years from the beginning of the seven-year peace agreement, plus however many years the earlier Seal judgments and rise of the Antichrist take.

- A seven-year period (but not the specific time of the Great Tribulation) is established first by reference to Dan 9:27. The latter week of his seventy weeks, which clearly relates to Revelation, can be symbolic only of seven years, giving sufficient time for events to occur. The 'time and times and half a time' of Dan 7:25 and 12:7 was understood by early Judaism as three-and-a-half years.
- The seven years in Dan 9:27, broken halfway way through by the 'abomination of desolation' as the text indicates, gives us two sets of three-and-a-half years which must constitute the seven years of the peace treaty time frame. However, *in addition to this*, another set of three-and-a-half years can be established (see below) for the period of the Trumpet judgments and the ministry of the Two Witnesses. This gives a total of ten-and-a-half years consisting of two overlapping time frames of seven years each, not including the indeterminate period of the early Seal judgments before the seven-year peace treaty is made.
- The Seal judgments *must* follow the Rev 4–5 throne-room scene in which the scroll with the seals is given to Christ to open. They are opened in Rev 6.
- The first four Seal judgments (an intensification of the troubles of the Difficult Labour period) lead up to the fifth Seal judgment. No specific time frame is given for them but they can be partly matched to the first three-and-a-half years of the seven-year 'peace' period, i.e., Antichrist's rise to power culminating in the setting up of his idol in the third temple. However, since there is no clear time frame given, there may well be more than three-and-a-half years of the first Seal judgments. This uncertainty (however many years plus three-and-a-half) gives

time for the Antichrist to establish his power base, gain the reputation of being undefeatable in war (Rev 13:4) and begin construction of a third temple as part of a global peace plan. His reputation and power combine to enable his authorisation of such a controversial project as the building of a third Jewish temple. However, the temple plan may have been in process even before the hidden rapture. If so, it will be a straw in the wind for those who are alert to the signs of the times.

- The fifth Seal judgment infers an intense persecution of the saints corresponding to the Antichrist's desolation of the temple. The cry of the souls under the altar in Rev 6:9–11 is most probably an indication of a slaughter accompanying the incident.

  The subsequent persecution to the death focuses on resisting, but as yet unbelieving, Jews (Rev 12:13–16). There is also a secondary focus on Jewish and Gentile saints (Rev 12:17) who, forewarned, left Jerusalem and probably Israel before the abomination of desolation.

- The persecution of the saints is also spelled out in the excursus (which is Rev 12), describing the attempt to destroy the woman and her child and God's protection of them for 1,260 days (three-and-a-half years). There seem to be two possible interpretations of the material.

  1. If we assume that the three-and-a-half-year period of protection (Rev 12:6) lasts until the final deliverance after the Trumpet judgments, then a hiatus of three or so years must occur between the initial attack of the Antichrist and the establishment of a protected settlement at Bozrah (the likely location). This gives another supporting time frame for the first part of the seven years of the Great Tribulation which is also the latter three-and-a-half years of the Seal judgments, after the abomination of desolation.
  2. If, on the other hand, the three-and-a-half-year period of protection immediately follows the betrayal, the Antichrist

may be permitted to attack the refugees at the end of that time during the Trumpet judgments. This would be a good reason for the Lord to fight at Bozrah on their behalf after or contiguously with the Armageddon battle.

I incline to the former interpretation. Of course, this part is more speculative, and there is more than one way of arranging these biblical events to suit the biblical data—this just seemed the most likely one for this particular period of time.

- The latter three-and-a-half years of the Great Tribulation's time frame (the Trumpet judgments) are identified in the Revelation 13:1–18 excursus, specifically in verse five where the Antichrist 'was given authority to continue for forty-two months.' This makes sense: The Antichrist has been ruling as a despot for the three-and-a-half years of the latter Seal judgments but now, after the Lord's open advent in the clouds and sending of the Two Witnesses, he is permitted to continue only so that the Lord's purposes for redemption can be fully worked out. At the end of this time Satan and the Antichrist overplay their hand by destroying all the saints and the Two Witnesses, who have the status of plenipotentiary ambassadors. This is only a pyrrhic victory for the Antichrist. Far from preventing the Lord's return in power, they will precipitate it, providing the final justification for the ultimate invasion and holy war against Satan and his followers.
- The Trumpet judgments seem to be preceded by the open parousia of Christ enthroned in the clouds, when he openly raptures all the saints (Matt 24:31, 40–41; Mark 13:27; Luke 17:34–36). Since the scriptures clearly show a rapture of saints alive on earth at the time, this cannot be the same event as the return of the Warrior King after the Bowl judgments, who has all the saints following him. Many commentators agree that the Antichrist has destroyed the whole believing church on earth, the Two Witnesses last of all, by the time of the Bowl Judgments (e.g., Rev 11:7; 12:7; 13:7, 10; 14:12–13; 16:6; 17:6; 18:24; 19:2). So, there would be no one alive to

take up from the earth at the return of the King riding the white horse ready for battle. In fact, *all* the saints will be accompanying him. The global intensity of the Bowl judgments and the frequent blasphemous statements of unrepentance by the earth-dwellers at that time make it highly unlikely there are any saints left alive.

No mention is made of the Two Witnesses and their extraordinary ministry and testimony during the Seal judgments or the early reign of the Antichrist. Nor are there any apparent links to them; but there are clear links during the Trumpet judgments. If we apply Dan 9:24 strictly and the *one week* is the last of the seventy weeks appointed for this age, then the Lord's return in the clouds, seated on the throne just before the Trumpet judgments, completes this age and begins the penultimate phase of the fulfillment of His work. It also marks the end of Daniel's seventieth week, which includes only the first half of the Great Tribulation. So, the three-and-a-half years of the Trumpet judgments, although they are the latter part of the Great Tribulation, do not count as part of the *seventieth week* seven-year period (Dan 9) since Christ ends that era at his open return and with the sending of the Two Witnesses. The witnesses are the forerunners of the New Era, just as John the Baptist was an Elijah forerunner in Jesus' time, and Elijah's return with Moses (assuming they are the Two Witnesses) can be similarly understood as the fulfillment of Mal 4 v. 5: 'Behold, I will send you Elijah the prophet before the coming of the great and dreadful day of the lord.'

- If the Trumpet judgments follow the Seal judgments chronologically as an intensification of judgment, which is the most obvious literal interpretation, then clearly more time is required during which the Two Witnesses testify and the Trumpet judgments occur. The time frame is given specifically by Rev 11:1–2 which suggests that the Two Witnesses have taken possession of the temple itself, but the nations led by the Antichrist still control the outer court and city. The time frame of forty-two months given for the control of the

Holy City by the Antichrist and his forces parallels the 1,260 days of prophesying by the Two Witnesses (Rev 11:3), presumably the same time frame. The duration of the Trumpet judgments and therefore the ministry of the Two Witnesses can also be deduced from the text of Dan 12:6–7. Their ministry concludes with their death and resurrection, after the annihilation of all the saints. Daniel 12:7 gives a three-and-a-half year time frame preceding these events, which must end the period of the Trumpet judgments.

- The time period for the Bowl judgments which complete the wrath judgments (Rev 16:17: 'It is done!') is not specific, but the judgments are so intense that it must be short for anyone to survive to contest the Rider on the white horse and his army at the battle of Armageddon, let alone leave survivors to be ruled by the saints during the millennium. The quick demise of the Babylon system (Rev 17:12, 16; 18:10, 17, 19) also supports a brief time frame for the Bowl judgments.

Beginning of Birth Pains	**The Difficult Labour**	**Minor Tribulation—Seals**	**Great Tribulation (GT)—Seals**	**Great Tribulation—Trumpets** **Babylon and Bowls**	**The Preparation and Training of the Saints for an Eternity of Service**	**One New Man in a New Creation** ***The beginning that should have been***
c. 30AD–c.2000AD?	Begins c.1948 or later?	? years plus three-and-a-half years	Three-and-a-half years	Three-and-a-half years	1,000 +? years	Into eternity
Began with founding of the Church Ends with birth of Antichrist? Or rebirth of Israel? Or both? We can only guess.	Beginning uncertain— Ends in the heavenly court's initiation of Just War (Rev 4–5) and the Hidden Rapture, which is **Parousia phase 1**	Begins after the Hidden Rapture The 'Minor' Tribulation: a prelude to the GT	Begins with the abomination of desolation, causing war in heaven. Satan cast to earth The Great Tribulation: Part 1	Begins with **Parousia phase 2** and the Open Rapture The Great Tribulation: Part 2	Marriage Supper of the Lamb Return of the King: **Parousia Phase 3** Armageddon Nations, Beast etc. judged The Millennium: Christ, the King of kings, rules on earth for a thousand years.	End of the universe as we know it The Great White Throne The New Heaven and the New Earth The New Jerusalem

		Seal Judgements begin (1–4)	Seal judgments continue and conclude (1–6)	Trumpet judgments Ends with death of all saints, Bowls of wrath, Armageddon war and the final phase of the Parousia	Followed by Gog-Magog 'war' and Satan's judgment.	Eternal Dominion (Final State) Holiness
		?	**Seven-year peace agreement** Daniel's seventieth week	The Lord's return in the clouds (**Parousia: Phase** 2) The Two Witnesses appointed as plenipotentiary ambassadors		
		Global Revival 1	**Seven-year period of the Great Tribulation** Global Revival 2			

Table 1: *Summary of the Last-Days Synopsis*

GLOSSARY

Abaddon—The beast that ascends from the bottomless pit in Rev 11:7 is most likely the same as the 'angel of the bottomless pit' in Rev 9:11. This angel is identified as Abaddon or Apollyon, a name which signifies death and destruction in both Hebrew and Greek.

Abraham—The 'father of faith' for the Jewish people and Christians. In Gen 12:1–7 God makes a profound promise to Abram (as he was) that his descendants would inherit the land of Israel and the blessings of faith (and the curses for disobedience) would come through them.

Abyss, the—A dark, deep place of confinement for demons, the angels who rebelled against God.

acolyte—A devoted cult follower of a charismatic religious leader or system.

AI—Artificial Intelligence, used to describe electronic processing systems which seem to mimic human thought processes, but are often exposed when it becomes obvious they are simply sophisticated algorithms which mimic the thought processes and preferences of their programmers instead. Their real danger is that they become an excuse for inhuman actions against real people.

anathema—Something cursed and which is therefore to be shunned. In some religions a formal ban on association with ideas or people considered heretics or just beyond the pale.

anthropology—The scientific study of human culture and custom, often specialising in the past in the study of preindustrial cultures.

Antichrist—The beast of Rev 13:1ff which rises up out of the sea. It is a symbolic figure for a man who is given power, authority and a throne by the Dragon, that is, Satan. This person is called the Antichrist because he tries to put himself in the place of Christ as the savior of the world. He is clearly a distinct human figure, although possessed, to whom the system of Babylon, its seven kings and allies, and the ten 'kings yet to be' do homage. This would make him a psychotic demoniac of Brobdingnagian proportions.

Antichurch—An alternative term for the Babylon system which the Antichrist and False Prophet use to enslave the world in the last days. It will be centered in the cult of the Antichrist and is a blasphemous parody of Christ's true church, just as the Antichrist's life and attributes are a blasphemous parody of Christ.

Antiochus IV Epiphanes—A Hellenistic king who ruled the Seleucid Empire 175–64 BC. He attempted to impose Greek culture on the Jews, sparking the Maccabean rebellion, which is described in the apocryphal books of the Bible

antisemitic/antisemitism—A perception of Jewish people and culture which may be expressed as hatred through words or actions.

antithesis/antithetic—An opposite or strongly contrasting view or thing, e.g., hope is the antithesis of despair.

apostate—Someone who abandons their religious faith, often taking up an opposing view.

archangel—A very high-ranking angel in the heavenly hierarchy.

Archon—Based on a Greek word meaning ruler. Here a reference to Satan as a formerly high-ranking angel.

Armageddon—The place of the final battle in this age between the forces of light (the good angels and redeemed humans with Christ as their leader) and the forces of darkness (demons and the God-rejecting earth-dwellers with Antichrist as their leader). The literal location includes Carmel and the plain of Jezreel.

atheist—A materialist (usually) who believes there is no God or gods and predicates their life on that proposition.

Baal Shem—A Jewish term for a wonder worker who performs miracles through mastery of a mystical system like the Kabbalah. *Baal Shem Tov* means 'Master of the Good Name,' that is, the name of God.

Babylon/New Babylon—Name of the ancient city of the Babylonian empire in the second millennium BC. Referred to as a type of the sinful world and in reference to the future, eschatological global system of cultural, religious and economic control instituted by the Antichrist and False Prophet. In this story Babylon is rebuilt as a global center of religious and cultural control, New Babylon.

Beast, the—See *Antichrist*

Berber Bishop—A reference to Saint Augustine, 354–430 AD, Bishop of Hippo.

blasphemy—Any act or speech which denigrates the true nature of God to show contempt, disrespect or irreverence.

Bozrah—Various scriptures associate Bozrah, modern Buseira, with a or *the* battle of Armageddon in the last days. We understand it as a place of protection for Jewish people during the tribulation period.

Brobdingnag—The opposite of Swift's Lilliput, a place of giants that Gulliver encounters on his journeys.

burner phone—A cell phone used for only one purpose and then discarded, so that the user cannot be tracked electronically. They may also be used for backup or occasional use.

Cherubim—The plural Hebrew form of the highest class of angel (cherubs) who among other things, guard the way to the Tree of Life and prevent mankind from returning to Eden. Satan was a cherub before being cast down for his prideful rebellion against God.

Christ—A Greek form of the Jewish term *Messiah*, meaning an anointed one, implying kingship. Depending on the user's interpretive framework it may refer to the literal, historical person of Jesus Christ, or an abstract idea or principle such as a *Cosmic Christ*.

chthonic—Relating to primeval conditions or those of the underworld in mythology.

Church, the—The body of Christians who profess faith in Christ. It can be divided into those who have a genuine faith and those who do not actually believe in Christ or his birth, death and resurrection but remain in the organisation for social, cultural or personal reasons.

Citadel, the—Reputedly the world's largest data centre facility owned by Switch located near Reno, Nevada.

contextualisation—Understanding something in its context in time and space or in its literary context.

conversion—A process initiated by an outside force which we choose to participate in, which may upend our worldview and priorities in life. Conversion can occur for the better or worse.

Cosmic Christ—See *Christ*

Delator—In ancient Rome a delator was basically an informer who could get a reward, often a share of the accused person's property, if the accused was found guilty. If the accused person were found to be innocent then the delator suffered the same punishment that would have been visited upon the accused person if found guilty.

demon/demonic—Demons are malevolent fallen angels whose ostensible mission is to destroy the human race and where possible to get them to participate in their own destruction.

Deplorables—A term made infamous by Hillary Clinton when she unwisely used it to describe all supporters of her opponent, Donald Trump. The implication was that those so designated were all uneducated, unintelligent rednecks who were morally reprehensible. It became something of a badge of honor for those who opposed her.

disappearing—See *Rapture*

distantiation/distantiated—The process of becoming aloof from something, or losing faith in it. A problem often faced by theological students overwhelmed by the sheer volume of critical views they might encounter which undermine their personal beliefs. In biblical study becoming aware of the *otherness* of the Bible with respect to how we see the world.

Dragon, the—A biblical term often used to describe the Devil, Satan.

earth-dwellers—A phrase used in Revelation to describe the reprobate who refuse to repent during the Great Tribulation judgments.

elect—Those people who are chosen by God for a particular purpose or for salvation itself.

Elijah—The OT prophet who opposed the corrupt kings of his day and was notably taken up to heaven in a fiery chariot. He is supposed to return at the end in Jewish and Christian understanding and many suppose he will be one of the Two Witnesses of Revelation.

emanation—The flow of something from a first reality, usually becoming a lesser reality with each step away from the original. In many of the heretical gnostic systems of thought the universe is composed of many emanations from God, some higher, some lower.

eschatology/eschatological—To do with the *last days*, from the Greek word *eschatos*, literally meaning 'last things.'

eternal dominion—My dynamic term to replace the passive term *final state*. It describes the active nature of our eternal existence in the future New Heaven and New Earth based in the New Jerusalem.

False Prophet—The person described in Daniel and the book of Revelation who supports the Antichrist/Beast666 through a process of deception of the masses.

fatalism—A philosophical teaching that subjugates everything to fate, leading to a counsel of despair that anything might improve.

Fedayeen—A militant group, usually Muslim, willing to sacrifice their lives for the cause of Islam and related political causes, such as the Palestinian cause in Israel. They are often characterised as terrorists but their supporters prefer the term freedom fighters.

Filastin/Filastini/Falastini—The Arabic base of the word *Palestinian.*

geopolitics—The analysis of power in international relations as it affects and is affected by geography.

Gog-Magog—A term used in this story to describe those who attack Israel and Jerusalem at the end of the millennium.

Golem—The Jewish prototype of the Frankenstein monster. A creature of clay which is brought to life magically, often with the purpose of righting some wrong against Jewish people, but prone to exceeding its mandate in harmful ways.

gospel—The *Good News* about Jesus Christ and the salvation he offers through his birth, death and resurrection and his second coming.

Great White Throne/Last Judgment—The final judgment of all after the millennium and before the creation of the New Heaven and New Earth.

Hadassah/Scopus, Hadassah/Ein Kerem—Two hospital sites in Jerusalem. Hadassah is the Hebrew name *Esther*, associated with the myrtle tree and something hidden, but named after her for her actions which saved many Jewish lives, as recorded in the Book of Esther.

Ha Ophel—The road which runs below the east side of the Temple Mount.

Hatzlacha/behatzlacha—A Jewish saying meaning *good luck* or *go with success.*

Helios—Greek for the sun.

Hell/Gehenna, She'ol/Hades—Refers to the underworld of the Dead (She'ol and Hades), and the place of demons, fire and destruction (Hell and Gehenna).

hermeneutic/s—The interpretation of the Bible. Depending on the text we may take different modes of interpretation, for example literal compared to allegorical or symbolic.

Hohhot—A major Chinese data centre in Mongolia.

Holocaust/Shoah—The attempt by the Nazis to make Europe *judenrein*, (lit. 'clean of Jews') ultimately by exterminating the race. Roughly two thirds of all European Jewry were destroyed, about six million people.

Iblis—Islamic term for Satan

Ichabod—A biblical character whose name means 'the glory has departed' (from Israel), named at birth after the capture of the Ark of the Covenant by Israel's enemies.

imminence—The doctrine that Christ can return at any moment and that no predicted event must intervene before that return. Most interpreters hold a form of this doctrine, but dispensational premillennialists and other literal interpreters apply it the most rigorously.

immortals—In this story a reference to those who have been through the first resurrection of the faithful at either the hidden rapture, the second coming, or later.

indenture—A form of servitude often not far removed from slavery where one serves for a period of time for a fixed return.

Ishtar's Gate—In ancient times the eighth gate to the inner city of Babylon and reconstructed for an exhibition in New York in 2019–20. Named after the Babylonian 'Queen of Heaven,' goddess of love, war and fertility.

Jeroboam and Uzziah's curse—Jeroboam's arm withered and Uzziah was struck with leprosy when they tried to usurp the priestly function in the temple by burning incense themselves. A worse fate befell Aaron's sons who tried to do the same thing in the Tabernacle.

Julian the Apostate—The Roman emperor who reigned 361–63 AD and who tried to turn the Roman empire back to a form of paganism, which was Neoplatonic Hellenism.

Lake of Fire—The place created for the fallen angels which is the ultimate destination of all reprobate.

latter rain—A farming term used in scripture (Joel 2:23; Jas 5:7) which is used to describe an outpouring of Holy Spirit in the last days.

left behind—A term used in this story to describe those who have made a profession of faith in Christ but have either not really believed or who have fallen away from faith. They are left behind on earth at the hidden rapture and have to undergo the various judgments of the tribulation times. Many will repent and still be taken up at the second coming of Christ.

limbo—A place which is supposedly an interim place between heaven and hell where souls who do not deserve the condemnation of Hell await the final judgment.

Logos—A Greek reference to Christ ('the word') who spoke all into existence.

Madame Defarge—A memorable character from Dicken's *A Tale of Two Cities* who sat knitting next to the guillotine.

Mark of the Beast—A physical mark, described in Rev 13:16–17, which is used in the last days to identify those permitted to engage in commerce. It is somehow associated with the 'number of the Beast.'

Marriage Supper of the Lamb—A celebration of Christ with all the saints after all believers, Jew and Gentile, have been destroyed in the Beast's holocaust of the faithful, last of all the Two Witnesses.

mene, mene, tekel parsin—The phrase written on the wall by a disembodied hand in Dan 5 to describe the judgment of the Babylonian king, Belshazzar.

Messiah—The Jewish word for the *Anointed One* who would be the savior or liberator of the Jewish people. *Christ* is simply Greek for 'anointed one,' so sometimes written Jesus the Christ.

Messianic Jew—A phrase used to describe Jewish people who have believed in Yeshua as Messiah and Lord, that is, the Jesus of the New Testament/Covenant.

mezuzah—A scroll in a special container placed at the right side of doorposts in Jewish homes.

miasma—A noxious or poisonous atmosphere associated with swamps which, in the Middle Ages, was thought to carry the Black Death.

millennium—A thousand years. Refers in last-days scriptures to an apparently literal thousand years of Christ's rule after Armageddon.

Milton, John—A preeminent English poet, historian and political activist of the seventeenth century whose most famous work is *Paradise Lost*.

minor tribulation—See *tribulation*

Mt. Scopus—A mountain in modern, NE Jerusalem.

Nazarene—An early term used to describe Christians based, of course, on Christ and Nazareth, the town he grew up in.

nemesis—An apparently undefeatable enemy.

nihilism—The belief or philosophical doctrine that existence and values are meaningless, which logically makes violent political action and terrorism pointless. But nihilists often also reject traditional reason as a value.

Nostradamus—A French astrologer of the sixteenth century famous for his prophetic writings.

Olivet—A term for the Mount of Olives in Jerusalem.

omphalos—A Greek term for the navel, used to refer to the center of the world.

Pan-demonium/pandemonium—A term coined by John Milton (lit. 'all the demons/devils') to refer to the capital city of Hell.

Parthian shot—A term used to describe a cavalry technique of mounted archers made famous by the Parthians, now synonymous with the term 'parting shot.'

plenipotentiary—A formal term used to describe someone invested with the full powers of a sovereign or powerful leader who commissions them to achieve some goal.

Poesy—A term used to describe the art and practice of writing poetry, or just poetry itself.

postmodern—A twentieth century movement rejecting assumptions and values of modern philosophy (that is, from the Enlightenment on) such as the possibility of objectivity, the validity of reason, the accepted meaning of progress, and the possibility of universal truth.

preternatural—Something extremely unusual, transcendent or supernatural.

prophetic perfect—A tense used in many biblical prophetic sayings which uses a past tense to describe a future event, as though that event had already happened.

pseudoscience—Statements, understandings and actions that claim to be scientifically objective but are not. This may be distinguished from specious science which may have all the trappings of real science in an accepted context, but has been perverted to political, social, or cultural ends, becoming effectively unfalsifiable and therefore not true science.

pyrrhic victory—A term meaning an apparent victory which will ultimately prove to be a stepping stone to defeat; for example, winning a battle but losing the war because of a massive depletion of forces in achieving the victory.

rapture (hidden and open)—Significant eschatological events in which the elect/faithful are taken physically out of this world without dying while being transformed, healed and regenerated in the process.

ratiocination—The process of deductive reasoning.

shalom—A Hebrew word for peace, harmony, prosperity, and wholeness.

She'ol—See *Hell*

Sicarii—A faction of Jewish zealots during the Roman occupation of Israel up to 70 AD; named after the small concealed daggers they carried.

social credit—A system of social control for rating and blacklisting nonconforming individuals being implemented in China in modern times. Not to be confused with the redistributive economic system of C. H. Douglas.

Sodom and Egypt—Here used in the same sense as Rev 11:8, a reference to the corrupted city of Jerusalem under the Antichrist.

Talmud—A collection of writings and discussions concerning the full extent of Jewish law and its application.

Tanach/Tanakh—The acronym used to describe the Jewish Old Testament: *Torah* (Law), *Nevi'im* (Prophets) and *Ketuvim* (Writings).

Tribulation/Great Tribulation/Minor Tribulation—Periods of great natural and social disturbance in the last days, particularly caused by God's judgment on the world but exacerbated by Satan and the Antichrist.

Uriel—One of the four archangels who serve God in the Jewish and Christian traditions.

Valley of Jehoshaphat—The wide valley between Jerusalem and the Mount of Olives in which the Garden of Gethsemane lies on the slopes of Olivet.

Yeshua/Jesus—The Hebrew and Greek forms of Jesus Christ's name, which is related to Joshua and Yehoshua and refers to salvation and deliverance. *Yeshua ha Mashiach* means Jesus the Messiah, that is, Jesus Christ.

Zealots—A religious and political movement in first century Judaism which sought to overthrow the Roman occupation.

www.ingramcontent.com/pod-product-compliance
Lightning Source LLC
Chambersburg PA
CBHW051138020726
47501CB00005B/1563
* 9 7 9 8 3 8 5 2 2 6 2 7 6 *